PUFFIN BC

THE DAUGHTER FROM A WISHING TREE

Sudha Murty was born in 1950 in Shiggaon, north Karnataka. She did her MTech in computer science and is now the chairperson of the Infosys Foundation. A prolific writer in English and Kannada, she has written novels, technical books, travelogues, collections of short stories and non-fictional pieces and several bestselling titles for children. Her books have been translated into all the major Indian languages. Sudha Murty is the recipient of the R.K. Narayan Award for Literature (2006), the Padma Shri (2006), the Attimabbe Award from the Government of Karnataka for excellence in Kannada literature (2011) and most recently, the Lifetime Achievement Award at the 2018 Crossword Book Awards.

Also in Puffin by Sudha Murty

SUDHA MURTY

THE DAUGHTER FROM A WISHING TREE

Unusual Tales about Women in Mythology

Illustrations by Priyankar Gupta

PUFFIN BOOKS

An imprint of Penguin Random House

PUFFIN BOOKS

USA | Canada | UK | Ireland | Australia
New Zealand | India | South Africa | China

Puffin Books is part of the Penguin Random House group of companies
whose addresses can be found at global.penguinrandomhouse.com

Published by Penguin Random House India Pvt. Ltd
7th Floor, Infinity Tower C, DLF Cyber City,
Gurgaon 122 002, Haryana, India

First published in Puffin Books by Penguin Random House India 2019

Text copyright © Sudha Murty 2019
Illustrations copyright © Priyankar Gupta 2019

11 10 9

This is a work of fiction. Names, characters, places and incidents are either the
product of the author's imagination or are used fictitiously and any resemblance
to any actual person, living or dead, events or locales is entirely coincidental.

ISBN 9780143442349

Typeset in Dante MT Std by Manipal Technologies Limited, Manipal
Printed at Thomson Press India Ltd, New Delhi

www.penguin.co.in

To John Shaw,
for believing in the power of women

Contents

YATRA NARYASTU PUJYANTE RAMANTE TATRA DEVATA

Preface

When I decided to write a book about women in mythology, I began my research and soon felt disappointed and disillusioned. I found that there is minimal literature that highlights the important roles that women have played. The most popular of these women are, without a doubt, Draupadi from the Mahabharata and Sita from the Ramayana, and then there's Parvati, who portrays a strong character of a goddess well-versed in the art of slaying demons and protecting her devotees. In fact, many rivers in our country are considered to be goddesses. However, the number of stories that abound about these women is strangely far fewer than the number of stories that speak about men. The literature that does exist is frequently repetitive and women are usually cast as subordinate or minor characters and remain underappreciated.

Perhaps this is because our society has traditionally been a male-dominated one, or because mythology has been written mostly by men, but most likely, it is a combination of these two reasons.

A popular sloka goes:

Yatra naryastu pujyante
Ramante tatra Devata

It means that god resides wherever women are respected.

However, if you look with sensitivity at the world around us, you will find that this is usually not true—whether you are a woman or a goddess. This is why I have, through this book, tried my best to retell stories that I grew up listening to and reading over the years, in an attempt to bring out the lives of some powerful women.

These stories have several recurring mythological figures that have featured in the previous three books in this series: *The Serpent's Revenge: Unusual Tales from the Mahabharata*; *The Man from the Egg: Unusual Tales about the Trinity*; and *The Upside-Down King: Unusual Tales about Rama and Krishna*. Readers can refer to these if they'd like to know more about certain characters that appear in this book.

I would like to thank my long-time and dear editor Shrutkeerti Khurana, and my wonderful support group at Penguin including Sohini Mitra, Arpita Nath and Piya Kapur.

My loved reader, I hope that you will enjoy these stories.

Introduction

The Trinity consists of three gods—Brahma, Vishnu and Shiva, and each has his consort.

Saraswati is the consort of Brahma, the creator. She is the goddess of knowledge and fine arts, usually depicted wearing white, playing a veena, holding a string of prayer beads (*japamala*) and a book, and smiling. A swan, her vehicle, is often shown alongside her. She's a peaceful goddess who is worshipped in many countries. Saraswati is also known as Vagdevi, the goddess of speech, and her blessings are sought by orators and writers, as she represents knowledge and education. Saraswati is a woman of few words and keeps a distance from conflict and controversies.

Lakshmi is the short-tempered consort of Vishnu, the protector. She famously resides in his heart and has various forms. She is also seen in the two forms of Bhu Devi, which is Lakshmi's earthly form, and Sridevi, Lakshmi's form associated with money and prosperity. Lakshmi is usually depicted sitting on a red or pink lotus, adorned in a red sari. She is said to be very disciplined and meticulous. When Lord Vishnu decided to take ten avatars on earth to protect dharma, Lakshmi had said to him, 'Dear husband, you are taking the avatars voluntarily with the sole purpose of upholding the righteousness of the

world. But you know that the two doorkeepers to our abode
here in Vaikuntha—Jaya and Vijaya—have been cursed to
take the human form on earth for three lifetimes and be your
enemy in those births. These two happenings are not just
a coincidence.'

Vishnu had smiled as Lakshmi continued, 'First, you will
take the form of the boar Varaha and kill Hiranyaksha, an
avatar of Jaya. Then, you will become Narasimha and slay
Hiranyakashipu (or Vijaya). Finally, you will kill Ravana
and Kumbhakarna in the form of Rama, and Shishupala and
Dantavakra in your human birth as Krishna. This means that
you will take four avatars to slay Jaya and Vijaya in their three
lifetimes. Lord, I will accompany you in a few avatars in my
different forms, and I will be the trigger for the destruction
of the three lifetimes of our doorkeepers. This way, I can
ensure that they fulfil their destiny.'

Subsequently, Lakshmi took the forms of Bhu Devi
during Vishnu's Varaha avatar (Hiranyaksha's killing),
Sita during the reign of Rama (the slaying of Ravana) and
Rukmini in the time of Krishna (the killing of Shishupala).

Finally, there is Parvati, who is the consort of Shiva, the
destroyer. She is known by multiple names—Durga, Shakti
and Sharvani among many others. She is seen as a fierce and
just goddess whose strength is often called upon for protection
and benevolence. She is almost always represented riding a
tiger or a lion and sporting a red sari. Parvati is Shiva's 'true'
consort, as she is considered to be his 'half'—both physically
and mentally. She is a great dancer, and Shiva is her teacher.
Even today, a couple dancing well is often referred to as
Shiva and Parvati.

Saraswati Bhagawati

The Source of Knowledge

When Brahma, the creator, decided to craft this world and everything in it, it was somewhat untimely, as chaos reigned supreme. To his disappointment, he was unable to focus on the work at hand and yearned for two things: peace and a knowledgeable companion who could assist him—a true partner. For such a task, his confidant needed to be intelligent, quiet, wise, well informed about arts and culture and have great control over the tongue and the mind.

Brahma spoke his thoughts aloud and to his unexpected delight, a beautiful woman with a sweet smile appeared in front of him, almost as if she had been created from his words. She wore a white sari and had four arms—two of her hands carried a veena and the other two carried a book and a japamala each.

Brahma was very pleased. 'I am grateful for your arrival and your assistance. I will call you Saraswati, Vagdevi or Vani,' he said. 'You are the master of knowledge and communication, and these names represent those qualities. All my creations will worship you as the goddess of knowledge, wisdom, art and speech.'

Together, Brahma and Saraswati began to work at their abode, Satyaloka, also called Brahmaloka.

Time went by, and soon, the battles between the devas and the asuras began. The two groups were constantly at war with each other. After many defeats, the asuras realized that the gods were winning most of the battles because of the Book of Knowledge, which lay in the custody of Saraswati and was given to her by Brahma.

One day, while the goddess was immersed in playing the veena in Satyaloka, the asuras stole the Book of Knowledge from her and ran away to earth.

When Saraswati found out about this foul play, she used her powers to track down and follow the asuras. Upon reaching earth, Saraswati realized that unlike other goddesses, she wasn't a warrior and didn't possess any weapons. So, the goddess of knowledge and learning decided to use her expertise. She concluded that the best way to catch the asura thieves was to take the form of a gurgling river and drown them.

Now transformed into a powerful river, she began flowing speedily towards the asuras. With the river water close on their heels, the asuras realized that they would drown if they didn't pick up speed. So, they abandoned the book on the banks of the river and ran as fast as their feet could carry them. Saraswati, happy to have the book back in her possession, did not pursue them.

While Saraswati prepared to return to Satyaloka, learned sages in the area learnt of her presence and of the famed book through their yogic powers. They hurriedly came to see her. Upon seeing Saraswati in her original form, the Book of Knowledge in her hand, the sages prayed to her, 'O Mother, we are helpless without you. You are our goddess. Won't you remain with us on the earth to help?'

Saraswati gave an enigmatic smile. 'I must go back to Brahma and assist him with his work. But I hear your genuine prayers and will allow a small portion of my power to continue flowing as a river in my name. This same river will later join the goddesses Yamuna and Ganga at Prayag, and the area of confluence—where we all meet—will be known as Prayag Raj. After that, I will lose my identity and my waters will merge with that of the Ganga.' Saying thus, she disappeared. And so, the River Saraswati flows on the earth.

She is also known as Guptagamini, since she is said to run beneath the ground surface in some places.

Andhaka, the son of Sage Kashyapa, became a great and powerful asura. One day in the heavens, he chanced upon the celestial Parijata flowers in the garden of the king of the gods, Indra. Seeing their beauty, he wanted to steal the tree from the heavens, and Andhaka began pursuing Indra incessantly for the Parijata tree. Indra, unable to take the pressure, ran to the Trinity for guidance. As the Trinity looked at each other, three colourful energies emanated from them: from Brahma, white (part-Saraswati); from Vishnu, red (part-Lakshmi); and from Shiva, black (part-Kali, a form of Parvati). The three energies merged to form a divine and brightly illuminated female form, and now this goddess was ready to go forth to successfully slay Andhaka.

Brahma, Vishnu and Shiva were extremely pleased and said to the trinity of goddesses, 'The three of you can protect all the creatures in the world. Henceforth, you will be worshipped twice a year for nine days each—once during Sharad Navratri, which will be in the winter and the other in the spring, which will be known as Vasanta Navratri. You will be worshipped by the names of Shakti, Vaishnavi, Kali, Chamundi, Durga and Saraswati, among others, and each of you will be worshipped on a different day. For instance, a day for Saraswati will have her worshippers thank her with items that bring knowledge to the world, such as books and musical instruments. This will be a special time for all students seeking Saraswati's blessings.'

Today, Navratri forms a big part of the lives of people all over the country, and children continue to worship Saraswati on the day of Saraswati Puja to request the goddess for knowledge and her blessings.

Narayani Namostute

The Eight Forms

Lakshmi, the Hindu goddess of wealth, fortune and prosperity, is a very popular deity in religions, such as Buddhism and Jainism, and in many countries, including Nepal and Tibet.

The goddess came to life in the famous mythological tale of the Samudra Manthana, or the churning of the ocean, where she emerged as a beautiful woman. Hence, her father is considered the king of the ocean. After Lakshmi's birth, all the beings around her—devas, asuras, humans and gandharvas—gazed at her in awe because of her striking beauty. Her father said, 'Dear daughter, just look around you. All these powerful beings are waiting for you to select a husband. You are in a unique position of choosing whomever your heart desires. Anyone you pick will be ecstatic to be the chosen one. As your father, I will perform your wedding rites.'

Lakshmi nodded and took a garland of flowers in her hands. While looking around, her eyes fell on Vishnu. Something in her heart propelled her towards him. She was attracted by his appearance, his calm demeanour, his stature and the elegant ornaments he wore. She placed the garland around his neck and became his eternal consort.

Vishnu was happy to have Lakshmi as his bride. He promised her, 'O Lakshmi, daughter of the king of the ocean, you are the light of the three realms. I will treat you with respect and keep you in my heart.' And so, Lakshmi settled in Vaikuntha, the abode of her husband, Vishnu.

One day, when the famed sage Bhrigu came to Vaikuntha, he saw Lord Vishnu sleeping and not doing anything useful. Out of rage, he kicked him on the left side of his chest—the same spot where Lakshmi resided. The goddess became upset at her husband's lack of action when he did not rebuke the sage. Being an independent thinker and an uncompromising wife, she left Vaikuntha and went to Karvirapura, known today as Kolhapur. Vishnu grew lonely in Vaikuntha and came down to earth, later settling in Tirupati.

Lakshmi's shadow, Alakshmi, also emerged with her during the churning of the ocean. Alakshmi embodies the opposite qualities of Lakshmi and always accompanies her. The arrival of Lakshmi to one's home brings prosperity to the family. However, if the family takes her for granted or does not respect her, Lakshmi leaves the house, but her shadow continues to reside there until the family's fortune and relationships are in ruins. Once this mission has been accomplished, Alakshmi travels to the next place of residence and joins Lakshmi.

Lakshmi manifests in eight different forms, which is why they are called Ashtalakshmis. In some temples, Lakshmi is displayed with sixteen hands, indicating all her eight forms at once.

The first, called Adilakshmi, is her earliest manifestation who emerged from the ocean. In this form, she is a kind

entity who wears a red sari and grasps a red or pink lotus. The second, Dhaanyalakshmi, is frequently worshipped by farmers and is represented with the deity's hands filled with grains as she pours them on to the ground. Dhairyalakshmi, the third form, is known for her courage and is worshipped by people facing obstacles who seek bravery and strength. The fourth form, called Gajalakshmi, is a common sight in temples: she is shown sitting, as two elephants pour gold or spray water on her. Santaanalakshmi, the fifth manifestation of Lakshmi, is usually surrounded by children and is worshipped by childless couples. Vijayalakshmi, the sixth form, is worshipped for the wealth of victory and courage. In the old days, before kings would depart for war, they would pray for Vijayalakshmi's eternal and consistent presence in the battlefield. The seventh form, Vidyalakshmi, as the name suggests, indicates the wealth of knowledge and education. She is different from Saraswati who is much steadier in her presence. The eighth form, or Dhanalakshmi, is the goddess of wealth, depicted with gold pouring from her hand.

In India, Lakshmi is a venerated goddess, and people worship her through many of her forms, depending upon their heart's greatest desires.

The God with the Head of a Horse

In his quest for eternal life, Hayagriva, an asura king, believed that if he prayed to the Trinity for the nectar of immortality, they would certainly try to trick him in order to not reveal their secret to him. So, he decided to pray to the goddess Shakti.

For many, many years, Hayagriva worshipped her with absolute love, focus and devotion. When she finally appeared before the devotee, Shakti refused him the nectar, denying his request for immortality.

Angered by this, Hayagriva thought, 'If I have to die, I must make it very complicated and almost impossible.' He wanted to outsmart the goddess, so he said, 'Mother, if I must depart this world, only a person with the same name as me and who possesses the body of a god and the head of a horse should be able to slay me.'

Shakti smiled and nodded.

Now, Hayagriva was convinced that this was as good as being immortal, for he did not think a creature such as he described existed. Believing he would never die, the clever asura continued his evil ways, inflicting cruelties on others with force and vigour.

The brutal king's subjects suffered and spoke to each other in worried whispers. 'How can there be a being with the same name, a god's body and a horse's head? Hayagriva will never die!'

Finally, they went to Brahma for help.

Brahma, however, had no solution. So, he approached Shiva, who suggested that they go to Vaikuntha to meet Vishnu.

When they reached the lord's abode, they found a standing Vishnu fast asleep. He was so tired after a particularly fierce battle with the asuras that he had fallen asleep standing and still holding his bow, Saranga, in his right hand.

Brahma was reluctant to wake Vishnu but knew that he had no choice. So, he created a colony of white ants and positioned them on Saranga. He thought the ants would eat the thread of the bow, causing a loud sound as the thread snapped and the bow opened. But he was terribly mistaken. The ants ate the thread in the blink of an eye, and the bow opened up with so much force that it beheaded Vishnu! His head flew up in the sky and fell with a splash in the middle of the sea.

Brahma and Shiva were not prepared for this. Alarmed, they looked in shock at each other and wondered what to do. Unable to find a way out of this situation, they prayed to Shakti. Soon, she appeared and said, 'Do not worry. Vishnu will be fine.'

The two lords looked incredulous.

With a smile, Shakti disclosed the reason. 'One day, Vishnu and Lakshmi were speaking to each other, and Vishnu had taunted her, "O Lakshmi! Just look at your relatives—your father is the ocean himself, yet nobody

can drink a sip of his salty water. What a waste! And what do I even say about your brothers who emerged with you from the churning of the ocean? Chandra, the moon god, is healthy for two weeks and then sick for the following fortnight. Halahala turned out to be the poison that turned the great Shiva into Neelkanth, the one with the blue throat. Amrut, the nectar of immortality, caused a great war, and your other brother, the seven-headed horse Uchaishravas, is constantly galloping around."

'Lakshmi was deeply offended. "It is very easy to talk ill of people," she said to her husband. "The world survives today because of my father. Chandra gives his light to the earth at night, and Shiva was able to save the world thanks to his blue throat. Amrut is the reason for the gods' eternal existence, and everyone desires a horse because of Uchaishravas. Maybe in time you will understand what it means to be a horse."

'So, you see,' Shakti concluded, 'Vishnu was predestined for a moment like this. This has all been designed to initiate the destruction of Hayagriva.'

Shakti grabbed a sword and beheaded a horse grazing nearby. She took his head and put it on Vishnu's body, which came back to life. 'The lord's body with this horse's head will be known as Hayagriva. *Haya* itself means horse, and now is the time for him to fight the asura.'

Vishnu, now in his form of Lord Hayagriva, followed Shakti's instructions and killed his namesake asura. When he came back victorious after the battle, the horse's head was replaced with his original one.

This form of Vishnu, also known as Hayashirsa, is one of the Dashavataras and is sometimes considered to be an alternative to the avatar of Balarama. He is usually depicted with four hands, carrying a Sudarshana Chakra. In this form, he is offered a unique dessert, also called Hayagreeva, which is made with chana dal—a type of lentil.

Shive Sarvaartha Saadhike

The Power of Faith

A long time ago, there lived an able and just king named Dhruvasanti who ruled the kingdom of Kosala. He had two beautiful wives, Manorama and Leelavati, who each had a son named Sudarshana and Shatrujit. The boys were only a month apart in age and were raised in a lifestyle befitting their royal status.

One day, the king went to the forest to hunt and was unexpectedly killed by a lion. Shocked by the unexpected loss, the people of the kingdom mourned their king's death.

Tradition dictated that Sudarshana, who was the older boy and Manorama's son, ascend the throne. However, Yudajit, Leelavati's father, strongly felt that his grandson, Shatrujit, was better suited for the crown. Yudajit was a clever king, and after some thought, he arrived in Kosala with his army to invade the kingdom's capital city of Ayodhya in an effort to make Shatrujit the new crown prince. Virasena, Manorama's father, countered the attack and stormed the city with his own forces in support of his grandson Sudarshana. The two sides battled each other and Virasena was killed.

When Manorama learnt of her father's death, she became terrified. She was certain that her son's life was in danger in Ayodhya, so she escaped with him. On the banks of the River Ganga, a revered sage named Bharadwaja took pity on both the queen and the young prince and provided them with care and shelter.

With Sudarshana nowhere in sight, Shatrujit safely ascended the throne and became the king of Kosala. One day, Yudajit, Shatrujit's grandfather, learnt that Sudarshana was under the protection of Bharadwaja. He thought of killing him so that the first-born prince could not pose a threat to the throne. However, the kingdom's wise ministers advised him not to proceed with this plan while the boy was under the hermit's protection.

In the hermit's ashram, Sudarshana heard a fascinating mantra one day. However, later, he could recall only the first word of the mantra and began chanting it repeatedly: *Kleem Kleem*. Little did he know the word signified the sacred Devi.

Years went by and the chanting became a part of Sudarshana's daily routine. Devi, who had finally noticed the young boy and his innocent devotion, appeared before him. She blessed him with a divine bow and arrow and promised her protection to him.

Meanwhile, Sasikala, the beautiful princess of Kashi and an ardent devotee of Devi, heard about Sudarshana and Devi's blessing to him. Instantly, she felt a connection to him and fell in love, despite never having met him.

Subahu, Sasikala's father, had arranged her *swayamvara*—a grand gathering of prospective husbands from whom the bride

would choose a groom—and invited many princes to attend. But Sasikala abruptly informed him that her groom would only be Sudarshana. This upset her parents. Sudarshana was a prince without a kingdom and any supporters, but what dissuaded them most was his powerful enemy and half-brother, Shatrujit. They advised Sasikala, 'Please, dear daughter, you must change your mind for the sake of your future.'

Sasikala, however, remained firm, unwavering in her decision. Reluctantly, Subahu sent a trusted messenger to the forest to invite Sudarshana to the upcoming swayamvara, though the princess's parents still hoped that one of the other princes attending the event would change their daughter's mind.

On receiving the invitation, Sudarshana grew eager to attend the event. But his mother, the queen-in-exile Manorama, stopped him, afraid of what lay ahead. 'O my dear child, please don't go!' she said. 'I know you have received a royal invitation, but it was sent just days before the swayamvara. That, in itself, implies that you are not an important suitor for the princess. I am sure that Shatrujit will also be there, and I don't want to lose you the way I lost my father.'

Sudarshana smiled. 'Mother, please don't worry. Devi is with me. I belong to the clan of warriors, as do you. It is perfectly acceptable to be afraid, but it shouldn't stop us from pursuing our path. We must push ahead.'

'But you are my precious son,' remarked Manorama sadly. Sensing that her son would not let this go, she said, 'Well, if you must go, then I will come too.'

Sudarshana agreed, and soon, the mother and son journeyed to Kashi.

When they reached, King Subahu welcomed them with great respect, honour and hospitality.

The next morning, Sudarshana ran into his half-brother, Shatrujit, at the swayamvara. Shatrujit was accompanied by his grandfather Yudajit. 'Why are you here?' Shatrujit asked, barely hiding his contempt. 'This is not the place for you. You don't even have an army!'

'I am here with Devi, and hers is the only support I need,' responded Sudarshana.

Just then, Sasikala entered the hall with a garland. Softly, she said to her unhappy parents standing nearby, 'I don't know how many princes have come here today expecting my hand in marriage, but the truth is that it doesn't matter at all. My decision has already been made. I am going to marry Sudarshana.'

The helpless and anxious king knew that he had to call off the swayamvara immediately. He made a loud announcement. 'My daughter has decided to marry Sudarshana. Hence, the swayamvara will no longer take place. We welcome you as our esteemed guests, and I request each of you to accept a few gifts. Please have a meal with us before you journey back to your own kingdoms.'

Yudajit became livid. He yelled, 'If your daughter had already chosen Sudarshana, why did you invite the other princes? This is an insult to all of us and I will not tolerate it. I am going to abduct your daughter and force her to marry my grandson Shatrujit.'

King Subahu grew pale. His army was no match for the strength and skill of Yudajit's forces! So, he turned to his daughter. 'My dear child, do you see the situation you have put us in? I beseech you, please change your mind and peace will prevail.'

'I'm sorry, dear father, but I must abide by my decision,' responded Sasikala. Undeterred, she approached Sudarshana and garlanded him, indicating to the guests present that she was now betrothed to him.

In an instant, the hall turned into a battleground, as Yudajit and Shatrujit's soldiers attacked the kingdom's guards with great force. The other parties joined one of the two sides, and the battle seemed like it would never end.

Suddenly, Devi appeared in the room out of nowhere, mounted on a ferocious tiger. She wore a red sari, sported a garland of mandara flowers around her neck and had weapons clutched in her multiple hands.

It was almost as if Sudarshana instinctively knew what to do next—he brought out his divine bow and began shooting arrows in quick succession.

When the soldiers in the room saw Devi, they put their arms down and retreated. Yudajit, however, too caught up in his desire to slay Sudarshana, did not recognize her. To him, she was just a woman. He roared at his soldiers, 'Why are you cowards fleeing at the sight of a woman? Surround Sudarshana and kill him!'

With a slight smile and without a word, Devi killed both Yudajit and Shatrujit with her perfectly aimed arrows.

This story of Devi's power and her execution of justice quickly spread everywhere.

In due course of time, Sudarshana was crowned the king of Kosala. He remained a devotee of Devi and dedicated one day a year in his kingdom to the goddess.

The Goddess of Fruits and Vegetables

There once lived an asura named Ruru who belonged to the lineage of Hiranyaksha. A devotee of the Trinity, Ruru performed a penance to please Brahma.

When Brahma appeared before him, he asked Ruru, 'What do you desire, my dear child?'

'O Lord, will you bless me with the boon of always having the Trinity protect my family?'

'So may it be,' blessed Brahma and vanished.

Time passed, and Ruru's son, Durgamasura, an ambitious and intelligent asura, grew up to be a powerful king. The guru of the asuras, Shukracharya, advised Durgamasura to pray to Brahma. Shukracharya knew about some of the foolish boons the asuras had asked for earlier, so he warned Durgamasura, 'Be careful what you ask for.'

Durgamasura listened to his teacher carefully before he departed for his penance. He meditated for years until Brahma appeared and asked him, 'What do you want, my devotee?'

Durgamasura was aware of the importance of the Vedas and the yagnas and decided that, unlike his predecessors, he did not want to ask for immortality. Instead, he said, 'Lord, you are the creator of the four Vedas. Please give their sole ownership to me.'

Brahma agreed and blessed Durgamasura.

Once he became the owner of the Vedas, Durgamasura kept them under lock and key in Patala, the lower realm of the earth. As a result, future generations of priests and sages, who were unable to refer to the Vedas, could not perform yagnas. Gradually, fewer yagnas took place, and the share of food usually offered to the fire to please the gods through yagnas became minimal. With the passing of some more time, the practice of yagnas became extinct. So, the gods grew disconnected from humans and began losing their power over the earthly realm, becoming weaker and weaker.

Durgamasura knew that the weakness of the gods would in turn enhance his strength. He soon began troubling the citizens of earth and other living beings on the planet.

Varuna, the god of water, became so thin and weak that he was unable to send rain for the people on earth, resulting in all the water sources drying up. Famine ravaged the world. Animals began dying due to the lack of food and resources, and so did the men, women and children.

However, Durgamasura showed no sign of change or repentance. As a king, he still demanded all resources from his subjects, including water, and was unbothered by the difficulties faced by his people. Instead, he used this opportunity to march towards the heavens, dethrone Indra and crown himself the king of the gods. This made all the gods, including Varuna, his slaves.

The gods felt helpless because of the Trinity's promise of protection to Durgamasura's father. Brahma had no inkling that giving the Vedas to Durgamasura would result in the end of yagnas, which would lead to powerless gods and famished people on earth.

Gods and humans alike became terrified of Durgamasura and his next move. Brahma and Vishnu ran to Shiva, requesting him for assistance.

Shiva was calm. He said, 'The Trinity has promised to protect Ruru's family, which is why we cannot declare war against Durgamasura. The only person who can do so is my wife, Parvati, who is independent of me in thought and action. Even though we have promised to protect the family, perhaps Parvati can assist. She is a fierce warrior who can easily defeat her enemies.'

Hearing the endless pleas of gods and humans alike, Parvati came down to earth on a lion. She was armed with sixteen weapons in each of her sixteen hands. The goddess observed the sparse vegetation and the heaps of dead animal and human bodies because of the never-ending drought. A mother at heart, she could not contain her sadness, and tears spilled from her eyes. The moment the tears touched the earth, they instantly turned into full-fledged rivers. When Parvati realized that her tears were turning into water, she used her powers to replicate one hundred eyes all over her body. This gained her the name Shatakshi—a hundred eyes.

Soon, the earth was blessed with water, but there were no trees left to sustain life. Parvati wondered how this problem could be solved. She knew that rainwater was the purest water of all and that it helped grow food quickly.

So, she went in search of Durgamasura. The asura king became enchanted with her beauty the moment he saw

her without realizing who she really was. He asked her, 'O beautiful lady, what do you want from me? I am sure that I can give you whatever you are looking for.'

'Release the Vedas and allow yagnas to resume. Let Varuna send water to the earth. Only rain can bring crops. Rivers can help but rain is essential.'

'I will agree to this, fair maiden. But I want you to marry me.'

'Don't you know that I am the wife of Shiva and the mother of the universe? Don't you know the meaning of love?' She continued, 'You have done wrong, my child. Stop your negative actions and understand that it is important for the world to have peace.'

Durgamasura, however, did not heed her words. He was obsessed with her beauty. He said, 'It is wonderful to know that you are Shiva's wife. But I must advise you to leave your ascetic husband who resides in a godforsaken place like Mount Kailash. Become my queen and I will be your slave for life.'

Parvati became furious at his words, as the gods watched the proceedings with interest and fear. 'There is no point in trying to explain anything to you,' she said. 'So, the only solution is that you must meet your end—maybe that is your destiny and the purpose of your words. Come, let us fight.'

Durgamasura laughed loudly. The thought was absolutely absurd to him. 'Oh, come on. How can a delicate woman like you fight a mighty demon like me?'

Parvati refused to back down, so Durgamasura reluctantly agreed to a fight. A terrible and fierce battle ensued. Parvati, now in her angry and vengeful avatar, used all her weapons and strategies and killed Durgamasura.

Gradually, Parvati returned to her calm and peaceful self and said to the gods and humans who had come to thank her, 'The form in which I fought against Durgamasura will be known as Durga. To save the world, I will give the seeds to grow plants, trees and vegetables, and Varuna will send rain to help cultivation. For this purpose, you must pray to me in my form as Shakambhari, with vegetables, and not flowers or ornaments. I will create a beautiful garden here, which will have vegetables growing in it forever. For this, I will be known as Banashankari, or the goddess of the garden, and I must always be dressed in green.'

Today, the temple of Banashankari is in the Bagalkot district of north Karnataka and has a statue of Parvati with a pleasant face, sixteen hands and riding a lion. During Navratri, she is decorated with garlands of lemons, chillies, eggplants, paan leaves and other green vegetables. On one of those days, she is offered only cooked vegetables, which must add up to the holy number of 108.

The Steps to Heaven

When King Pandu died, his widow Kunti went to Hastinapur with her five children, the Pandavas, to live with her husband's half-brother and the ruling king, Dhritarashtra; his wife, Gandhari; and their hundred children, the Kauravas.

Kunti, who was also known as Pritha, felt strongly that her children were princes in name only, since they did not have a father or a kingdom to inherit. In time, she began feeling like an unwelcome guest in her brother-in-law's house and wondered how long she was likely to stay there.

One day, the wandering sage Narada came to the palace and happened to see Kunti and Gandhari in conversation. Later, he asked the women, 'What were both of you discussing?'

'The welfare of our children,' said Gandhari.

'Then you must pray to Goddess Parvati. She is, after all, the best mother of them all,' responded Narada.

'I am aware of the might and power of Mother Parvati. But how do we pray to her for our children?' asked Kunti.

'Perform the Gaja Gowri puja. But it must be done in the month of Bhadrapada, prior to the Ganesha festival and at the end of the rainy season.'

'What must be done for the puja?' asked Kunti.

'Invite Parvati to your home. Her family should also come, if possible. She must arrive on an elephant. If that isn't feasible, you must bring an elephant, mount the goddess's statue on it and provide her with clothes, vessels and flowers. Pray to her to protect and care for your children.'

With these words, Narada said goodbye to Kunti and Gandhari.

After Kunti returned to her room, she sat down, worried. 'Gandhari is the queen and has a hundred children. She can easily get a real elephant. She can assign tasks to each child and perform the puja with great pomp and show. It is my destiny that I don't have such liberties or power. And my children are only five in number. What must I do?'

Meanwhile, Gandhari sat in her chambers and thought, 'I shouldn't invite Kunti to this special puja. She doesn't have any resources, and when she sees how I perform it, she may remember all that she lost as a queen and it will make her unhappy. I don't want to be the cause of her pain.'

Certain that she was doing the right thing, Gandhari performed the puja by ensuring the attendance of a real elephant, mounting the goddess's statue on it and offering plenty of delicious food and fabulous clothing.

When news of the puja reached Kunti, she felt dejected. 'Gandhari hasn't invited me because I am no longer of a status that befits her company,' she assumed.

When her sons saw her in such a state, they asked her, 'Mother, what is bothering you?'

'Gandhari performed the Gaja Gowri puja today for her hundred sons. She has so many sons to assist her. However, she didn't invite or inform me. I, too, wanted to perform the puja, but how can I do it given our situation?'

'Mother, the strength of your five sons is much more than that of a hundred men,' said Arjuna. 'Just as Mother Gandhari got a real elephant for the puja, I will bring for you the white elephant Airavata from Indra's court. In fact, I will ensure that Goddess Parvati herself comes for the puja.'

'How will you do that, my child?' asked Kunti.

'You don't worry yourself with that, my dear mother,' said Arjuna as he set out with his bow and arrow. He went to the outskirts of the city. After some time, he found an open space there and shot hundreds of arrows at the sky, carefully weaving a staircase of arrows leading to the heavens. Once the staircase was complete, Arjuna climbed the steps and entered the court of Indra.

A human entering heaven worried the gods sitting in the court. Now anyone would be able to walk into their abode and take away their wealth.

Arjuna announced his presence to all the gods. 'I am Arjuna, O respected ones, and I earnestly request a meeting with Indra.'

Indra recognized the brave, young warrior and asked him with affection, 'Dear Arjuna, what do you desire? I am ready to give you all you want, but ensure that you destroy the staircase after your work is done. You are a man of admirable character, but not everyone in the realm below is like you, and we do not want unsavoury characters entering our home.'

Arjuna bowed. 'My mother wants to perform the Gaja Gowri puja, and for that she needs an elephant. May I borrow yours?'

'Of course. You can take Airavata. Lead him down the strong staircase you have built,' replied Indra.

'Also, I would like all the materials needed for the puja.'

'Take whatever you wish,' agreed Indra.

'May I also request you to speak to Lord Shiva and Goddess Parvati and invite them to attend the puja in person?'

Indra smiled. 'Yes, I will ask them.'

Arjuna brought Airavata down to the earthly realm along with the necessary materials. During the auspicious time for the puja, Parvati arrived with her husband and their *gana*, or loyal followers. She sat on Airavata, and Kunti worshipped her with sincerity and devotion.

As the puja drew to a close, Parvati blessed Kunti. 'May your children's names always be remembered when people talk about dharma and good deeds. May your son Arjuna, who came all the way to the heavens to fulfil your wish, be known as Partha, or the son of Pritha.'

Today, the Gaja Gowri puja is performed in Karnataka for the welfare of children. It is usually done for sixteen days, during which a different type of food is made every day. This puja is not specific to any community, nor are there many rituals involved; it is only about faith and belief. Since it is not possible to get a real elephant these days, people keep an idol of Parvati on an elephant made of clay.

To War with a Woman

Once upon a time, there lived two asura brothers named Shumbha and Nishumbha, sons of the cruel asura Shambasura.

Together, the brothers prayed to Lord Brahma and performed a severe and austere penance in the holy place of Pushkara. After many years, the lord appeared. 'What boon do you desire, my devotees?' he asked.

The brothers were ready with their answer. 'Lord, we do not want to be killed by a male member of any species— whether it is a man, bird, animal or god.'

Brahma smiled and said, 'So may it be.'

The brothers were ecstatic. It was nothing short of a boon of immortality. The thought that there could ever be a woman powerful enough to slay them both didn't even cross their minds.

Shumbha was the king of the land and upon receiving the boon, the behaviour of the two brothers became unbearable— even more barbaric than they were as generals of Taraka's army when the mighty asura was alive. To make it worse, they were assisted by two great warriors named Chanda and Munda, who joined them with the sole purpose of serving the brothers.

In time, their atrocities reached their zenith, and the suffering of the common man became excruciating.

One day, Chanda and Munda were wandering around in the forest when they saw a lady so stunning that they immediately reported the news of her beauty to Shumbha. They told the king that the lady was fit to be his queen.

Shumbha, who trusted Chanda and Munda's opinion, sent a marriage proposal to this beautiful woman through two of his deputies.

The woman, who was a form of Goddess Parvati, rejected the request. 'I have taken a vow to marry someone who can defeat me in battle. So, I cannot accept the king's proposal,' she said to the envoys.

Shumbha, however, didn't give up. He sent other trusted ministers to convince her. However, they all came back with the same message.

At last, the king sent 60,000 soldiers to seize the woman, but Parvati, armed with multiple weapons and riding a tiger, killed all the soldiers and the asuras who approached her, including Chanda and Munda.

Shumbha and Nishumbha were dealt a huge blow with the death of their loyal servants. 'How dare she destroy our mighty army and kill our trusted warriors?' Shumbha thundered in rage. The brothers set out to fight her themselves, forgetting about the boon.

As it was destined, Parvati fought fiercely with incredible strength and honour, slaying the asura brothers and forever freeing their kingdom and the people from their evil reign.

Brahma's boon remained intact—the brothers had been slayed by a woman and not by a male member of any species.

The Woman of the Battlefield

Rambha and Karambha were two asura brothers who desired special powers. They began to seek these powers through deep meditation and prayers to Agni, the god of fire, and Varuna, the god of water. Rambha took residence in a blazing fire and began praying to Agni while Karambha stood inside a river and prayed to Varuna.

When Indra, the king of the gods, learnt of their penance, he grew worried. He desperately wanted to stop the brothers from obtaining any boons that could be used against the gods.

After much thought, Indra disguised himself as a crocodile, entered the waters in which Karambha stood in meditation and quickly attacked him, killing him on the spot. He then also tried to attack Rambha and drown him, but the asura managed to escape with the grace of Agni.

The years passed and Rambha was crowned the king of the asuras. Soon, he was also blessed with a son, whom he named Mahishasura. The baby's name, which meant 'buffalo-headed asura', referred to the fact that the boy was an asura with the strength of a buffalo.

When Mahishasura grew up, he came to learn of the story behind his uncle's death and became furious with Indra. Eagerly, he waited for the right time to wage a war against the king of the gods.

During the wait, he prayed to Brahma for the boon of immortality. Brahma could not give such a promise, so instead he blessed him with another boon. 'Mahishasura, your death will occur only at the hands of a woman.'

Mahishasura was satisfied. 'It is impossible for any woman to overpower a man of my strength,' he thought with arrogance.

When the right time came along, Mahishasura waged a war against Indra. The heavenly army failed to defeat their opponent, and all the gods were driven out of their abode. This forced the gods to come together and take action. They resolved to end Mahishasura's life. However, Brahma's boon prevented any man from defeating the feared asura.

So, the gods devised a plan. With the blessing of the Trinity and the combination of their powers, they created the asura's nemesis—a divine form of the goddess Parvati with multiple arms and beautiful long black hair.

The gods gifted this avatar of Parvati a red sari, gold jewellery and a magnificent crown. 'You will be known as Durga, the goddess of the battlefield,' said Brahma. In addition, they presented her with a tiger as her primary vehicle and gave her each of their characteristic weapons: the trident from Shiva; the Sudarshana Chakra, or discus, from Vishnu; a *kamandalu*, or small water pot, from Brahma; a bow from the wind god Vayu; arrows from the sun god Surya; a thunderbolt from Indra; a spear from Agni; and a conch from Varuna.

When Durga was ready, Brahma spoke on behalf of all the gods and requested her, 'O Goddess, none of us can kill the mighty and uncontrollable Mahishasura. You will need all of these weapons to slay him. We beseech you to help us.'

Almost as if those words were all that she had been waiting for, Durga went forth and battled fiercely with Mahishasura. It was on top of a hill known as Chamundi Hill that she killed him.

The area that Mahishasura ruled was known as Mahishamandala in the old days. It is now known as the city of Mysuru, which is in Karnataka. Parvati came to be known as Mahishasura Mardini or Chamundi. In Mysuru, there is a temple on the top of a hill dedicated to this fearless avatar of Parvati.

This story about Parvati is described in the religious text *Devi Mahatmya*, or 'Glory of the Goddess'. This legend became such an integral part of her worship that prayers were offered to Durga by royal families before the initiation of war. Even today, during the nine days of Navratri, Parvati is worshipped in all her different forms, such as Vaishnavi, Kali and Durga.

The Daughter from a Wishing Tree

Parvati, the consort of Shiva and the mother of Ganesha and Karthikeyan, felt lonely at times. Shiva was constantly in meditation, and her sons were usually busy with activities outside the home. Parvati felt the boys would never truly understand her and yearned for a daughter with whom she could share her feelings.

One day, after another bout of loneliness, she spoke to Shiva. 'I am terribly bored. Take me to the most beautiful garden in the world.'

Shiva smiled, glad to show her the celestial garden of Nandana at Amaravati, the capital city of Indra's kingdom.

There, Parvati saw many beautiful trees, but Kalpavriksha, the wishing tree that had emerged during the churning of the ocean, enchanted her completely. Suddenly, she had a desire to ask for a daughter who would take away her grief and loneliness. Her wish was immediately granted by Kalpavriksha, and she found herself with a beautiful baby girl. Affectionately, Parvati named her Ashokasundari—'a gorgeous damsel who reduces loneliness'.

Ashokasundari grew to be a young woman who was devoted to her parents. Parvati loved her dearly and enjoyed her cheerful company.

When she came of marriageable age, Parvati was of the opinion that only an earthly king of the stature of Indra would be an appropriate match for Ashokasundari. After much thought, Parvati decided that Prince Nahusha of the Lunar dynasty would be suitable and shared her view with her daughter, who was quite agreeable to the idea.

One day, Ashokasundari was enjoying herself with her friends in a nearby forest. The group of girls were laughing and talking loudly. This caught the attention of a demon named Hunda. When he saw Ashokasundari, he immediately fell in love with her. He approached her and asked, 'O lovely woman, I am Hunda, an accomplished asura, and I have completely lost my heart to you. Will you marry me?'

'I'm sorry, but I am going to marry Nahusha someday,' said Ashokasundari truthfully.

Hunda became enraged but did not display his true feelings. Instead, he hatched a plan.

A short while later, he disguised himself as a widow, whose husband he had killed earlier. In the form of the widow, he approached Ashokasundari. 'Hunda is a malicious asura and frequents this area,' the widow said. 'I am in this helpless state because of his cruelty. Young maiden, it is not safe for you to stay here. Why don't you accompany me to my ashram? I am poor and only have a small place, but please come and experience my hospitality.'

Ashokasundari agreed, told her friends that she would be back after some time and followed the widow to the ashram. The moment the two women stepped through the gates, Hunda shed the form of the widow and turned back into himself.

Realizing she had been tricked, Ashokasundari cursed him, 'O Hunda, you do not know who I am. I am the daughter of Goddess Parvati. I curse you to be killed by Nahusha.'

Ashokasundari fled through the open gates of the ashram and made her way to her parents' home in Mount Kailash.

Afraid of the curse, Hunda decided to take immediate action and kidnapped the unsuspecting young Nahusha from his palace and kept him under lock and key.

But as destiny had ordained, a maid took pity on Nahusha and handed him over to the famous sage couple Vasishtha and Arundhati, knowing that they would keep him in hiding and take care of him. When Hunda found out that his prisoner had escaped, he was livid and searched for Nahusha everywhere but was unable to trace him.

The sage couple took great care of the prince and made sure to educate him. Within a few years, the prince grew up to be a fine young man. He waited for an opportunity to slay Hunda.

Meanwhile, Hunda hatched another plan. He kidnapped Ashokasundari again when she was alone. He threw her into an empty room, and as he turned the lock in the keyhole, he said to her, 'I have killed Prince Nahusha.' Ashokasundari was dismayed.

The young maiden's grief overwhelmed her, and she wondered how her mother's belief that she would marry Nahusha could be wrong. She began to sob uncontrollably.

A Kindara couple—half-human and half-horse—happened to pass by Ashokasundari's window and heard her cries. They stopped and asked, 'O young lady, why do you cry so bitterly?'

'The mighty Nahusha is dead,' she said.

They smiled, amused at the thought. 'Please don't listen to such rumours, young maiden. Nahusha is alive and well. He is not an ordinary mortal, for he has been taught by the great sage couple Vasishtha and Arundhati. We are blessed with the art of face reading and can assure you that the two of you will be wed. Your children will be famous throughout this land.'

Ashokasundari smiled with gratitude, and her heart filled with hope again.

A few days later, Nahusha came in search of Ashokasundari and fought Hunda for her freedom. After a long battle, Nahusha killed the asura and married Ashokasundari to the delight of his subjects.

In time, he became such a powerful emperor that he could easily defeat the gods. He even dethroned Indra for a short period of time.

This story of Ashokasundari is not a popular one, but it shows Parvati's longing to have a daughter and her profound belief and knowledge that a daughter is indeed rare and precious—a discovery that people continue to make even today.

Yatra Naryastu Pujyante
Ramante Tatra Devata

The Maiden of the River

The River Ganga, considered to be of the feminine gender, is one of the most sacred and vital rivers in our country. It boasts multiple tributaries and flows down from the Himalayas, originating in the caves of Gangotri in Uttarakhand.

A mythological story surrounding the Ganga suggests that Vishnu took the avatar of a dwarf named Vamana and asked Emperor Bali for three feet of land, and that each step he would take must equal the size of one of his feet. After Bali agreed to what appeared to be a simple request, Vamana expanded in size until he became a giant called Trivikrama. With one foot, he occupied all of the land on earth, while the second occupied the sky. The third pushed Bali down. When the second foot occupied the heavens, Brahma recognized the foot to be that of Vishnu's and became thrilled at the opportunity to perform a puja for the lord. So, he took some water from his small kamandalu and washed Vishnu's foot. Once he did so, the water on earth began to flow like a river in the heavens, and the Ganga was created. This is why the river is considered very holy and is also called Devaganga.

Another story about the river involves the short-tempered sage Durvasa. The sage was once taking a bath in the Ganga in the heavens when, suddenly, a strong breeze blew away the cloth that he had been wearing. Ganga saw this and laughed. Durvasa became furious and cursed her, 'You are a river that resides in the celestial realm, but your immaturity displays your behaviour—similar to that of the humans on earth. From now on, you will reside on earth instead.'

Ganga realized her petty sin and apologized to Durvasa, who had by then calmed down. He said, 'I can't change the curse—you will flow on the earth—but I will give you a special power. Whoever takes a dip in your pure waters will be immediately cleansed of any sins they have committed.'

That is why people visit the Ganga in places, such as Haridwar, Prayag, Rishikesh and Kashi even today to absolve themselves of their sins.

There once lived a king named Bhagiratha who wanted Ganga to descend from the heavens to the earth. The king's ancestors had been reduced to ashes, and the only way for them to obtain salvation was for the River Ganga to flow over their ashes. After much prayer and penance to the gods, Ganga was allowed to flow on the earth, but she flowed with such force that she could have easily submerged the entire planet. So, Shiva decided to direct only a fraction of her flow to the earth by holding her in his *jata*, or hairdo, thus earning him the name Gangadhara. Yet, her force was so strong

that when she reached earth, the gush of the water flooded the ashram of the sage Jahnu. Jahnu became so livid at the destruction that he drank the river. Ganga was then unable to proceed further. Seeing that the river had stopped flowing, Bhagiratha prayed again, and soon, the river emerged through Jahnu's ears, thus earning the name Jahnavi.

A story about Ganga also speaks about Nandini, a wish-fulfilling cow and the daughter of the sacred Kamadhenu, who was given to the great Rishi Vasishtha's ashram to help him perform his prayers and to take care of his guests. One day, eight *vasus*, or minor gods, experienced Nandini's hospitality at Vasishtha's ashram, and came back and told their wives about her. The wives immediately wanted to possess the holy cow and insisted that their husbands catch Nandini and bring her to them. Prabhasa, one of the eight vasus, took the lead. He stole the cow and then directed the other cows out of the ashram. Vasishtha became furious when he learnt of the robbery and cursed the eight vasus. 'You will all take birth as mortals on earth as the punishment for your actions!' he thundered.

The vasus begged Vasishtha for forgiveness until he agreed to reduce the potency of his curse. 'May you all be born out of the holy River Ganga and be immersed in her immediately after birth. Then your sins will be cleansed. But Prabhasa, who stole Nandini, will remain on earth for a much longer time.'

This is why Ganga, who was married to a king named Shantanu in her human form and became the queen of Hastinapur, immersed her first seven children in water, freeing them from their human form and their lives as mortals. The last one, however, stayed on earth for a long period of time as Bhishma, the respected warrior in the Mahabharata.

Shantanu's story, however, goes back to times of yore. In that time lived a frog in a forest. This frog heard about the River Ganga and how people yearned to go on a pilgrimage to her to take a dip in her waters. So, the frog also decided to travel to the river.

Sadly, he got caught in a stampede during his journey and was crushed to death under a man's foot.

In his next birth, the frog took the form of a man who was employed by Indra, the king of the gods. Indra was very appreciative of his work and gave the man a cart full of gold.

Now that he had more than enough money to make the trip, the man again started his journey to the River Ganga. However, his bullocks died on the way and he was at a loss for how to continue further. He requested Surya, the sun god, for help. 'Lord, if you help me now, I will give you half of this gold.'

Surya assisted him and the man managed to make his way to the Ganga. Once he was there, he took a dip in the waters and donated all the gold he had by immersing it into the river.

A short time later, when Surya asked him for his share, the man was unable to pay. Surya, now angered, turned the man into a jackal as punishment. With no place to go, the jackal lived near the river and had a dip in the waters every day.

Time passed until one day Ganga showed up in the form of a beautiful maiden. Fascinated, the jackal followed her. Ganga, afraid of the animal, threw a stone at the jackal, which hit him and blinded him in one eye. Still, the jackal continued to follow her. She ran to a sage nearby and hid behind him, telling him about the stalking jackal. Upset, the sage ensured that his disciples killed the animal, burnt him and immersed his ashes in the river.

A few years later, the same ashes transported the seeds of a sal tree to the banks of the river. Eventually, a huge tree grew there. The sage, through his yogic powers, realized that the jackal's ashes were responsible and were a part of the tree. He immediately instructed his disciples to cut the tree down. So, they fell the tree until only the dry trunk remained. The sage then ordered his students to burn the trunk. Out of this fire emerged a handsome young prince, whom the sage named Shantanu. The sage said, 'Young man, for years you have tried to meet and be a companion to Ganga in different forms. I bless you with all my heart—you will marry her, even if it is for a short period.'

Much later, Shantanu met Ganga again, now in her human form, and became enchanted by her beauty. She agreed to marry him on the condition that he must never question her actions. Deeply in love with her, Shantanu accepted this condition. In time, she gave birth to seven children, whom she immersed in water after they were born.

On the birth of the eighth child, Shantanu questioned her, fearing the fate of the newborn. This questioning broke the condition upon which Ganga had agreed to marry Shantanu. She abandoned him but left the eighth child with him—this child was none other than the glorious Bhishma.

That was how Vasishtha's prophecy came true.

Usually, Ganga is represented in temples by a stone statue of a woman standing atop a crocodile and holding two pots of water. She is related to the Trinity very closely, since she was born from Brahma's kamandalu, washed over Vishnu's feet and emerged from Shiva's hair.

The point where other rivers meet the Ganga is termed Prayag. For instance, you will find Rudraprayag, Karnaprayag and Devprayag in Uttarakhand. Ganga also merges with the River Yamuna in Allahabad, and this point of confluence is known as Prayag Raj.

The Perfect Revenge

Shurpanakha, the sister of the powerful king Ravana of Lanka, was very beautiful.

When she came of age, she fell in love with Vidyujjihva, the prince of a different clan of asuras. She knew that her brother would not approve of this alliance, and so, she married Vidyujjihva in secret.

When Ravana learnt of her marriage, he was furious and wanted to punish her. However, his wife Mandodari encouraged him to respect his sister's choice, and Ravana finally came to accept Vidyujjihva and Shurpanakha as husband and wife. Little did anyone know that Vidyujjihva had married Shurpanakha only to get close to Ravana and murder him.

One day, Ravana went to visit his sister in her new home. To his disappointment, Shurpanakha was not there. Vidyujjihva seized the opportunity and attacked his brother-in-law, but he was no match for Ravana, who killed him quite easily.

Shurpanakha become a widow at a young age, and the incident created a gigantic misunderstanding between her

and her brother. She refused to listen to Ravana's side of the story. She truly believed that Ravana never really accepted her marriage and had punished her by killing her husband.

Shurpanakha began spending her days in the forests of Lanka. Time passed, but her thirst for vengeance against her brother only grew greater. The princess was part-asura and knew Mayavi Vidya, or the magic of illusion. She could transform into any form she chose.

One day, when Shurpanakha was on the banks of the River Godavari in Panchavati (or today's Nashik), she saw Rama, the exiled prince of Ayodhya, from a distance and lost her heart to him.

When she approached Rama and confessed her love for him, Rama instantly refused. When she insisted, Rama directed her to his younger brother, Lakshmana, who insulted her and cut off her nose.

The injured Shurpanakha backed away from the brothers but saw Rama's wife, Sita, standing nearby. She found Sita stunning. That was when it occurred to the asura princess that this was her chance—her unconquerable brother could not be defeated directly but through a creative plot. Knowing Ravana's weakness for beautiful women, Shurpanakha went to her brother and described Sita's unique beauty. Just as she had planned, Ravana fell into her trap and eventually abducted Sita.

The kidnapping made it certain that Rama would neither forgive Ravana nor let him off the hook. He was sure to kill Ravana, and he did.

It was the perfect revenge.

The Frog Who Forgot Happiness

A long, long time ago, there lived a group of sages who went out every morning for their prayers and came back to their dwellings in the evening. They led a pious and simple life, eating fruits and drinking water from a nearby well. A frog, who lived in the well, observed their way of life and also turned pious.

One day, the frog saw a poisonous snake entering the well while the sages had gone for their prayers. The frog knew that if the sages drank this water, they would die. So, he waited impatiently near the well till the sages returned. When they came near, the frog jumped into the well to warn them about the poisonous water. The sages saw the sudden movement of the frog and peeped inside the well. To their astonishment, the frog was dead. When the sages fished the frog out from the well, they noticed that the colour of the frog's body had changed to bluish grey. That's when the sages realized that the water had been poisoned and through their yogic powers, they discovered that the frog had given his life to save all of theirs.

Together, they recognized the frog's sacrifice and blessed him. 'A simple creature like you saved us from certain death. O dear frog, we will revive you so that you can ask us for a boon.'

When the frog came alive, he said in a human voice, 'I want to be beautiful like Parvati and marry someone who is extremely learned and is an emperor.'

The sages smiled and said, 'May you take birth as a very beautiful and pious woman whose name will always be associated with virtues and devotion to your husband. You will grow up to marry a great and knowledgeable king.'

Thus, the frog was born in his next life as Mandodari, daughter of Mayasura—the architect of the asuras—and the celestial dancer Hema. Mayasura knew of his daughter's previous birth, which is why he named her Mandodari—derived from *mandook*, meaning 'frog' in Sanskrit.

As time progressed, Mandodari grew up to be an exquisite and pious woman. She eventually married Ravana, the greatest warrior of the time and a highly learned man.

Mandodari, however, forgot to ask the sages for happiness and never experienced true joy in her life. She experienced immense sadness at the hands of her husband, Ravana, who kidnapped Sita, another man's wife. Mandodari repeatedly advised her husband to release Sita but to no avail. The consequences of the abduction resulted in a great war, which led to Ravana's defeat. She also lost her great warrior son, Meghanada, in the tumultuous war.

In Indian mythology, we remember her has one of the five great women, or Panchakanya—Ahalya, Tara, Mandodari, Draupadi and Sita.

The Goddess of the White Lake

Bharata, one of the hundred sons of the first Tirthankara, ruled the kingdom of Ayodhya, while Bahubali, the youngest of the sons, got Podanapur.

One day, when he was in the armoury, Bharata saw a rotating circular disc that seemed to point in a certain direction. When he spoke to the astrologers of the kingdom about his observation, they said, 'This is an indication that you will rule the earth and become an emperor.'

In time, it seemed that the prediction was coming true, as Bharata fought many wars and expanded his kingdom with the aid of the disc, which pointed the way to him on his journey.

One day, Bharata was returning to Ayodhya after one such war, anticipating that he was close to becoming an emperor, when suddenly the disc stopped rotating.

Bharata knew that this was an indication of something important and sent inquiries to various scholars and astrologers. Finally, he was told, 'The disc has stopped because you also need your ninety-nine brothers to submit to you. Only then can you proceed on your quest to be an emperor.'

So, Bharata sent a royal letter to all his brothers, informing them that they must either submit to him or wage war against him to determine the winner. Ninety-eight of his brothers were absolutely displeased when they received the communication. For the sake of his ego and land, Bharata was calling his own brethren to battle. Given their limited resources, the ninety-eight brothers decided to give him their share of the kingdom and left.

Bahubali, however, refused to submit and surrender his share of the kingdom. Since he was a tall and strong warrior, he sent a message to Bharata: 'Come, brother. Let's fight— just the two of us. I don't want either of our subjects to be innocent victims, so let's keep this between us.'

Bharata agreed, and the two met on the battlefield.

The brothers engaged in three kinds of tournaments: Malla-yudha (wrestling), Jala-yudha (battle in water) and Drishti-yudha (staring at each other). Bharata was equal to Bahubali in skill, but Bahubali used the advantage of his height to defeat Bharata in the Jala-yudha and the Drishti-yudha.

When he won, Bahubali knew that he would be crowned emperor—the lord of many, many kingdoms. But the rush of power faded away just as quickly as it had come. 'I don't need this kingdom,' he thought. 'Look at us! The love for land and power has turned us into mortal enemies!'

With that intense realization, Bahubali gave away all that he had won to Bharata and left to meditate and perform a penance in the search for ultimate bliss.

He became a Digambar Jain monk and gave away all his clothes, money and ornaments. He stood bare naked for years in one spot, anthills forming around him. Even dust, water, the sun and the wind did not bother him. Despite his focus and dedication, he was still unhappy. It bothered him that he was standing on the land of his brother Bharata.

A year passed. Finally, Bharata felt ashamed and went to visit his brother. When the brothers reunited, Bahubali became free of all attachments and attained supreme knowledge and moksha. Bharata built a beautiful statue of his brother.

History differs from this account. This single-stoned fifty-eight-foot granite statue of Bahubali (or Gomateshwara) is located on top of Vindhyagiri Hill in Shravanabelagola in the Hassan district of Karnataka. It was built by the great Jain prime minister of the Ganga dynasty, Chamundaraya, and it represents detachment from worldly life. It is one of the rare statues that depicts Bahubali having a calm expression. Besides this, many of his statues exist in Karnataka alone, in places, such as Veluru, Karkala, Gommatagiri and Dharmasthala—but none can surpass the beauty of the statue in Shravanabelagola. Owing to this very beauty, Chamundaraya began regarding himself as the greatest man on earth. His perspective and ego thus dominated all his future work.

One day, the statue was washed with milk and water, and Chamundaraya ordered drums of milk for the ceremony of Abhisheka, or the anointment of the statue. He was surprised to learn that despite drum after drum of milk being poured

on the statue, the milk would not flow past Bahubali's hips. What was wrong? No matter how much the priests tried, the result remained the same, and the ceremony of Abhisheka remained incomplete.

Just then, Chamundaraya saw an old lady walking past with a small container of milk.

She asked him politely, 'Sir, may I use this milk for Bahubali's Abhisheka?'

'O Ajji, we are unable to bathe the statue despite the litres of milk that we have poured over it. But if you think your little bit of milk will help in successfully completing the ceremony, please go ahead and try.'

Slowly, the old lady went up the makeshift staircase until she reached the head of the statue and poured the milk over it. To everyone's surprise, the milk covered Bahubali's entire body. In fact, there was so much excess milk that it flowed down and formed a pond of white on the ground.

Chamundaraya knew then that she was no ordinary lady but a divine soul. When he apologized to her, she transformed into Goddess Yakshi and said gently, 'Don't be proud, dear one. Everybody has the faith they believe to be true. What you can accomplish with that faith is much more important than what you can do with money. I wanted to show you that, which is why I played this little trick on you.'

If you visit Shravanabelagola today, you can still see the pond below the hill. It was filled with milk once, and that's why it is known as Bilia Kola, meaning 'a white lake' in Kannada. And you will also find a statue of Ajji holding the little milk pot in her hand.

The Secret of Youth

Once upon a time there lived a king named Sharyati.

One day, the king went hunting in a forest nearby. His daughter, Sukanya, accompanied him with her friends, and they set up camp. The king became engrossed with the hunt and galloped away with some of his troop, so the young maidens decided to go for a stroll.

Sukanya stumbled upon a big white anthill with two shining holes. Surprised to see such an unusual anthill, she picked up a stick from the ground and poked the two holes. Instantly, blood started oozing out from the hollows. Scared, Sukanya turned around and headed back to the camp with her friends.

Inside the anthill lived a sage named Chyavana. He had been meditating for decades, and white ants had built their nest all around his body. The nest had two holes that were directly aligned with Chyavana's eyes. Princess Sukanya had, in her ignorance, poked the sage's eyes, which had instantly blinded him.

Chyavana was furious. Using his powers, he ensured that the call of nature come to a pause for the army of

the king responsible for this act. The curse went into immediate effect, and the soldiers and officers of Sharyati's army began suffering, unable to relieve themselves of their bodies' toxic waste.

Soon enough, the king realized the folly of his daughter. He approached Chyavana and begged for mercy. 'O respected sage, forgive my daughter for her unintentional sin. Do not punish my army for her mistake. Please tell me what I can do to make you happy.'

'I am an old man, and now, I am also blind because of your daughter's thoughtless actions,' said the sage. 'If you are here because you want me to retract the curse, your daughter must marry me and take care of me.'

The king was hesitant to give away his beautiful daughter in marriage to this old sage. Sukanya, however, came forward and said, 'Father, our army must not suffer because of me. I am ready to marry this sage and serve him.'

Chyavana was extremely pleased. The wedding took place and the curse was lifted.

Years passed and Sukanya continued to serve her husband sincerely.

One day, the Ashwini Kumars, the divine twin physicians, were passing by Chyavana's ashram when they saw the stunning Sukanya. They approached her and said, 'O lovely maiden, why are you living here with an old sage? Marry one of us and you will have a better life.'

'Sirs, I am sorry, but I will not leave my husband,' said Sukanya.

'Well, what if we bless Chyavana with the gift of youth? After we do so, you must honestly choose Chyavana or one of us with an unbiased and true mind,' one of them said, trying to tempt her.

At first, Sukanya rejected their offer and went to her husband to explain the situation to him. Chyavana asked her to call the Ashwini Kumars. When they met, the sage said to them, 'I accept your offer. Please give me youth.'

The Ashwini Kumars gave Chyavana a combination of three treatments—the sage first took a dip in a lake containing special herbs, then a herbal paste called *kayakalp* was applied to the sage's body, and finally, he was asked to eat a herbal mix.

Finally, the twins and Chyavana took a bath in the lake and came out looking not just youthful but also identical to each other.

Sukanya prayed with sincerity and identified her husband correctly. Chyavana was very happy and promised the twin physicians that they would get a part of every offering from him whenever he would perform a yagna.

The herbal mix that Chyavana consumed changed him into a young man, and this led to the coining of the term *chyavanaprash*, a concoction of herbs, spices, jams and oils that is eaten by many people today.

The Princess and the Ugly Dwarf

When the Pandavas were in exile for thirteen years, their spiritual teacher, Sage Dhoumya, used to sometimes visit to entertain and counsel them by telling them stories.

Frequently, Yudhishthira regretted having bet Draupadi in a game of dice and losing her along with his crown. When he finally shared this with the sage, Dhoumya said, 'Good times and bad are inevitable in the circle of life. During tough periods, people do things that are sometimes out of their nature. Even a sermon or an intelligent suggestion may not help. History is filled with stories of kings who have made such follies and caused their families to suffer. In all cases, people have managed to pass through the rough times. Hence, there can never be a permanently good or bad time in anyone's life.'

Yudhishthira was curious. He asked, 'But was there ever a foolish king like me who played a game of dice, bet his wife and lost his kingdom? I have caused grief to my family and my subjects.'

'Yes, there was,' said the sage. 'His name was Nala. Let me tell you his story.

'There lived a beautiful princess named Damayanti of the kingdom of Vidarbha. Her beauty was so renowned that even the gods could not help but admire her.

'The king of Nishadha kingdom had two sons—Nala and Pushkara. Nala was very handsome, charming and well respected.

'One day, when Nala went hunting, he stopped at a lake to rest. There, he saw many white swans in the midst of which there was also one beautiful golden swan. Nala couldn't resist this fascinating creature. He slowly approached the golden swan from behind and seized it. The surrounding birds immediately flew away, but this golden bird couldn't escape Nala's tight grip.

'To his surprise, the swan suddenly spoke to him in a human voice. "O great Nala! Please let me go. I need freedom, just like every living being on the planet. You are a great king, general and ruler, and I know that you will agree with me."

'Nala realized the truth in the swan's words. He loosened his grip to release the bird.

'"I am glad you did that," said the swan. "You have listened to a bird and done your duty as a compassionate ruler. When someone receives help, they should be grateful. So, in return, I will give you something. I will ensure that you get the finest match in this world. Princess Damayanti, the daughter of King Bhima, is celebrated for her beauty. Gods want to marry her and apsaras are jealous of her. Her loveliness is truly unmatched, even in the heavens. I give you my word that I will introduce you to her."

'Saying thus, the bird flew away.

'Deep in thought, Nala stood in silence, still processing this unexpected turn of events. He had indeed heard of Damayanti and felt ecstatic about the swan's promise.

'The swan made his journey to Vidarbha. He went to the royal gardens and hid behind a bush. Other white swans also joined him and cheerfully moved about in the gardens. Princess Damayanti was attracted to the white swans, but when she approached them, they all flew away.

'After some time, Damayanti spotted the golden-winged swan. She was enchanted and went close to him with the intention of catching him. When she approached the bird, he slowly moved away and lured her a short distance from her friends and guards, where nobody could see them. Then he allowed himself to be caught by the princess.

'The swan said, "O Damayanti, the most beautiful one, please release me. I am the messenger of Nala, the most handsome prince I have ever seen. No princess other than you is worthy of his valour and compassion. I have seen millions of couples, but most are mismatched. Nala and you are truly worthy of each other in every way. If you set me free, I will take your message back to Nala."

'The bird went on to describe Nala and his many outstanding qualities. Without realizing it, Damayanti began falling in love with this unknown prince. She set the swan free.

'A few days passed and Nala occupied Damayanti's thoughts all day and all night. She could neither sleep nor eat properly. She was a young woman utterly and desperately in love. When her father, Bhima, learnt of this development, he quickly arranged a big swayamvara and invited all the princes of the allied kingdoms to attend.

'Nala was delighted to get an invitation. He dressed his best, got into his chariot and started his journey towards Vidarbha. He was a skilled charioteer, possessing the ability to ride extremely fast. On the way, he saw four shining chariots and four handsome gods descending from the sky. The gods stopped Nala and one of them said, "I am Indra, the king of the gods. These are my friends—Agni, the god of fire; Vayu, the god of wind; and Varuna, the god of water. Though there are gorgeous maidens in the heavens, we heard of Damayanti's celestial beauty and couldn't resist it. So, we thought that at least one of us must marry her."

'Nala was dumbstruck.

"'O noble prince," they continued, "you are known for your wonderful manners, and hence, we want a favour from you."

'Nala recovered and replied, "Salutations to all of you. I am, after all, just a mortal. How may I help you?"

"'We request you to go to Damayanti as our ambassador of love. Describe our great qualities to her. Convince her that she must marry one of us. Explain to her that it is a privilege for a human being to marry a god."

'Nala felt hopeless and despondent. He replied with as much courage as he could muster, "I will help you and stay true to my word. But, my lords, Damayanti is always surrounded by her relatives and friends. So, how do I meet her privately to convey your desire and advocate your love?"

'The gods smiled with amusement. "Don't worry, Nala," they said. "We bless you with the power of invisibility so that you can fulfil our mission."

'Armed with his new gift, Nala stealthily entered Damayanti's chambers in the palace and waited for the right moment. When she was finally alone, Nala appeared in his true form.

'Startled, Damayanti asked, "Who are you?" She noticed his handsome form and continued, "Are you a human or a god? How dare you enter my chambers without permission!"

'"I am Nala, the prince of the Nishadha kingdom. I have come to you as an ambassador of the gods Vayu, Varuna, Agni and Indra. They are fascinated by your beauty and desire that you choose one of them at the swayamvara tomorrow."

'Damayanti smiled. "I am happy to see you, Nala. You have been on my mind ever since a golden swan told me about you. You are the man of my dreams, and I have given my heart to you. Then how can I marry one of the gods? Besides, I am a mortal and the gods are not."

'"O Damayanti, you are more beautiful than I ever imagined. But I don't have the power to go against the wish of the mighty gods. I have made a promise to them."

'"It is a swayamvara, Nala, and I will decide whom I will marry," said Damayanti firmly. "Please don't interfere."

'Nala used his gift of invisibility and left the palace. He met the gods, conveyed Damayanti's message to them, leaving them disappointed and wondering about what they should do next.

'The next day, all the princes came to the swayamvara. The four gods changed their appearances to look like Nala and sat near him.

'Soon, Damayanti arrived, holding a garland in her hands. She gazed at the princes in the audience, and to her astonishment, she saw five Nalas sitting next to each other. She realized that the gods had made a crafty move. She prayed to them, "O dear gods, I have the right to choose my husband today. You are indeed great souls. But if my love for Nala is true, you will show me mercy and give me the ability to see you in your real forms. If I am not with Nala, I cannot be happy with anyone and will never truly love any of you with my heart."

'The gods were touched by her tender plea. Instantly, Damayanti was able to differentiate between Nala and the four gods, even though they outwardly still appeared to be like him—she noticed that the four gods were not batting their eyelids, while Nala was doing so like all mortals.

'Smiling, she stepped forward and garlanded Nala. The four gods blessed the couple and gave boons to the groom.

'Indra said, "I promise to attend all your pujas and yagnas."

'"I will be with you whenever you call upon me," promised Agni.

'Varuna and Vayu also gave similar boons, and the gods left for their abode.

'On their journey home, the four gods met the well-dressed Kalee, the deity of degradation and depravity. "Where are you going?" the gods asked him.

'"I am off to Damayanti's swayamvara."

'"You can head back because Damayanti has already chosen Prince Nala," they said.

'Kalee was very disappointed and felt cheated. As he returned home, he promised himself that he would teach Nala and Damayanti a grave lesson sometime during their lives.

'Damayanti married Nala with great pomp and show. The world rejoiced at the perfect match. Damayanti accompanied her husband to the kingdom of Nishadha. Together, they had two children.

'Nala was a fair and just king, and he took care of his subjects and formulated strict rules about hygiene and health. The subjects were happy, and Kalee could not enter the kingdom for a long time as he could only make his way inside if there was a presence of dirt, bad habits and injustice.

'One day, Nala forgot to wash his feet before his evening prayers. Kalee seized the opportunity and entered Nala's body.

'From that day on, Kalee played games with Nala's mind, causing the king to begin losing his mental and physical health.

'Pushkara, Nala's brother, invited him for a game of dice. Nala usually refused such invitations, but this time, he accepted it under Kalee's influence on his mind.

'Damayanti was unhappy with her husband's decision. She kept telling Nala to change his mind, but he refused.

'When it was time, the game started.

'At first, Nala bet his army. When he lost, he gambled all his wealth and lost that too followed by the forfeiture of his kingdom in the third round. Kalee, happy with what he had accomplished, left Nala's mind and body. Knowing that Nala had nothing more to lose, Pushkara shamelessly said to his brother, "The kingdom is now mine. Leave. You are no longer welcome here."

'Damayanti then wisely arranged for her two children to be sent to her parents' home.

'Dejected, Nala knew that he must do as told. His subjects felt miserable about this turn of events but knew that they could not stand up to Pushkara, their new king.

'Nala told Damayanti to also return to her father's home so that she could live in comfort, but she refused. She insisted on living with him. So, the couple left the kingdom for a nearby forest. Nala knew that he had done wrong. Damayanti was a princess and a queen, and here she was with him, wandering through the forest without food. For a few days, the husband and wife survived only on water.

'One day, Nala saw some birds hopping about on the ground. He decided to catch the birds and sell them. This way, he could earn some money to buy food for his wife. So, he undressed and threw his clothes over the birds like a net. To his surprise, the birds held the clothes in their beaks and flew away. Now poor Nala had no clothes!

'When Damayanti found out, she felt terrible and gave Nala half of her sari so that he could at least cover himself.

'Together, they started walking until they came across an intersection of three roads: one to Ujjain, one to Vidarbha and one to Ayodhya.

'Nala again tried to convince his wife to go back to her maternal home. "Why don't you stay with your parents for some time? Our children are also there, and you will be comfortable. I will find a way to get our kingdom back. I promise to call you when I am ready."

'"How can I leave you here in the forest to fend for yourself? A husband needs his wife in tough times. I am going to stay with you through hunger, thirst, worry and work. We will share everything—the good and the bad."

'Nala fell silent.

'After walking some more, the couple decided to rest under the shade of a tree, and the tired Damayanti soon fell asleep.

'Nala was overwhelmed with grief. He remembered how his wife had rejected four gods and married him instead. And now, he had brought his wife to such a pitiable state! He was restless. He thought, "If I take her with me, who knows where this might end? She may suffer even more, and I won't be able to see her in that situation. This is not her fault; she doesn't deserve this. My best option is to leave her here at this juncture to Vidarbha and go my own way. If she doesn't find me when she wakes up, she will have no choice but to go to her parents."

'With a heavy heart, Nala left his beautiful wife sleeping under the tree and quickly walked away.

'When Damayanti woke up, Nala was nowhere to be found. She searched for him and eventually realized what he had done. She cried and sobbed, walking deeper into the forest in the hope of finding him. Suddenly, a python lunged at her and began to wrap himself around her. Desperate, Damayanti cried out for help. As luck would have it, a group of hunters nearby heard her cries and rescued her from the python.

'Later, she narrated her story to the hunters, hoping that they would understand her plight. To her dismay, the head of the hunters fell in love with her because of her ravishing beauty. She prayed in earnest, "O God, if the love for my husband is true, allow me to curse this man who stands before me. Let him be burnt alive!"

'With those words, the head of the hunters suddenly caught fire and died. The other hunters, who were witness to the incident, sprinted away.

'Aimlessly, Damayanti resumed wandering through the forest and lost track of time.

'One day, she encountered a caravan crossing the forest. The caravan stopped, and a man asked, "O noble lady, are you all right? What are you doing here in the forest?"

'Damayanti did not respond.

'The man said, "This forest is full of beasts and serpents. Our group is heading to the Chedi kingdom. Come with us and we will find something for you to do there."

'Without uttering a word, Damayanti boarded the caravan and journeyed forward with the group. Though the days passed, she did not reveal to them her status of a queen or talk about her husband who had gambled everything away.

'One fateful night, the group pitched their tents near a lake. A few hours later, elephants and wild beasts came on a rampage, destroying the tents and killing many people. Damayanti was one of the few survivors. She was now in complete shock—it seemed to her that a series of misfortunes was striking her and the people around her in quick succession. "Perhaps I am being punished for not listening to the gods," she thought.

'As if to validate her opinion, some people in the group began referring to her as a bad omen. Yet they took her along with them in the caravan, up to the city of Chedi.

'In the capital city, she was introduced to the queen mother of the kingdom as a lady in distress. The queen mother was kind to her. "What work can you do?" she asked.

'"I can be a lady-in-waiting to the princess, or a *sairandhri*," replied Damayanti.

'The queen mother nodded, and Damayanti was finally able to find a temporary home.

'Time went by and Damayanti continued to pray to the gods. She knew that her parents would take care of her children, but she was constantly worried about her husband.

'Meanwhile, Nala was facing challenges of his own after leaving Damayanti sleeping under the tree. He had wandered into another forest where he ran into a serpent with a circle of fire around him.

'Nala heard a cry. The serpent looked at him and said, "My name is Karkotaka. I am stuck here inside this circle of fire. Please help me out."

'Nala, being compassionate, rushed to help. He carried Karkotaka on his shoulders and brought him out of the circle of fire.

'Suddenly, Karkotaka bit him, and Nala was immediately transformed into an ugly creature the size of a dwarf. He became upset. "What have you done to me? How can you do this to someone who has helped you in a difficult situation? You are a wretched and ungrateful being."

'"Please don't curse me just because I have bitten you and made you ugly," said the serpent. "I have done this on purpose. You are in a miserable condition, and this way, no one will recognize you. Don't worry, you will have the power to transform back to your original form at some point."

'Nala kept mum. "Perhaps there is some truth to Karkotaka's words. Who knows what the future will bring?" he thought.

'The two parted ways, and Nala took the road to Ayodhya, where Rituparna was ruling the kingdom.

There is a place known as Karkotaka Hill near Bhimtal, in the state of Uttarakhand, with a serpent or Nag Temple located atop it. It is believed to be the place where Karkotaka met Nala and bit him in order to help him pass through that difficult period in his life. This holy temple is frequented by pilgrims who believe worshipping the deity of Karkotaka helps obtain protection from serpents.

'Nala changed his name to Bahuka and went to the court of the pious Rituparna. "My name is Bahuka, sire," said Nala. "I am an expert cook and can make the most delicious food for you in the shortest amount of time." Nala was able to do so because cooking requires fire, wind and water, and he knew he had the blessings of Agni, Vayu and Varuna.

'Rituparna tasted Nala's cooking and found him to be true to his word, so Nala was employed as the head chef in Rituparna's royal kitchen.

'Thus, Damayanti and Nala lived separately, not knowing each other's whereabouts. Meanwhile, Damayanti's parents were getting increasingly worried about their daughter with each passing day. They knew that Nala had lost his kingdom and that the couple were now in exile. Since they had not received any news from Damayanti, they sent messengers and soldiers to search for her. They even announced a reward

for whoever gave valuable information that would help locate the couple.

'Sudeva, one of the members of the search party, found his way to Chedi. There, he saw Damayanti serving the royal princess in the palace. When he got a chance, he approached her. "O my queen, you are the lady-in-waiting here, but I recognized you immediately."

'Damayanti earnestly inquired about the well-being of her children and parents.

'Later, Damayanti was called to the court in the presence of the queen mother and Sudeva. The queen mother was smiling. "O Damayanti," she said, "you are my niece! I neither came for your wedding nor have I seen you for a very long time. I apologize that I did not recognize you even though you have been staying with us. Please forgive me for treating you like a sairandhri. You can stay with us for as long as you would like."

'"Please do not be hard on yourself, my dear aunt. These things happen during difficult times. For a long time, I didn't want to go to my maternal home without my husband, but now I realize how worried my parents are about me. I still don't know where my husband is, and at this time, I'd prefer to go live with my parents and children."

'The queen mother showered Damayanti with many gifts and rewarded Sudeva with plenty of gold.

'Soon, Damayanti reached her parents' house. She was reunited with her children but remained unhappy. She knew that her husband was somewhere out there. So, she sent messengers to search for him by asking the people they came across a particular question: How can a man abandon his wife in the middle of a forest, use half of her sari to cover himself and then leave without thinking of her protection? Is he not an irresponsible husband?

'She received many responses. Almost all of them said, "Yes, the husband is irresponsible."

'But one unusual response caught her eye. It was from Rituparna's kingdom. It read: "It was a matter of fate. If the wife understands her husband's intentions, she will forgive him. He did it for the sake of his wife, so that she would be taken care of by her parents."

'In addition, the messengers said, "When we went to Rituparna's palace with the message, we met Bahuka, the king's confidant and the man in charge of the kitchen. He inquired where the message had come from. When he learnt that it came from Princess Damayanti, his eyes filled with tears and he asked about your welfare as well as your children's."

'Damayanti asked the messengers, "What does this Bahuka look like? Is he handsome?"

'"Madam, he is a dwarf and the ugliest person we have ever seen," came the reply. Damayanti was stunned, and she dismissed the messengers with a wave of her hand.

'For a long time, Damayanti deliberated on this piece of information. Her instincts were telling her that Bahuka was none other than Nala, but she was hesitant because of the description of his appearance. Finally, she devised a plan.

'King Rituparna was a skilled dice player. Since Bahuka was in his inner circle and spent much time with the king, he also learnt to play the game. Rituparna was excellent at counting the number of leaves on a tree, while Bahuka was skilled at riding chariots. In time, they learnt varied skills from each other.

'Now that Damayanti was keeping her ears open for news about Bahuka, she frequently received updates about the dwarf at Rituparna's court who was famous for cooking and riding chariots.

'One fine day, she decided to put her plan into action and shared the details with her father. "Father, please send a messenger to Rituparna's court to inform the king that my second swayamvara is tomorrow morning. If he arrives with Bahuka, I will see how to go further from there."

'The king was not convinced. However, he decided to trust his daughter's intelligence and sent a message to Rituparna.

'Rituparna had heard of Damayanti's beauty and was ecstatic to obtain an invitation. "Had they informed me earlier, I would have definitely attended. How will I reach in time for the swayamvara now?" he wondered out loud. Suddenly, he looked around for his confidant. "O Bahuka, you are my last resort. Can you get me there quickly? We can take our fastest horses and my best chariot."

'Nala felt extremely heartbroken when he heard the news about his wife's second marriage, but he couldn't refuse his master. He began preparing for the journey to Vidarbha with a heavy heart, and soon, the duo departed.

Rituparna and Bahuka reached the kingdom of Vidarbha the same evening. When Damayanti learnt that the king of Chedi was accompanied by the ugly dwarf, she knew that no one other than her husband would have been able to reach the kingdom this fast.

To test her theory further, she sent her children to meet Bahuka, who embraced them and wept intensely. That same night, she sent a message instructing Bahuka to cook for her. When she tasted the dishes, she recognized her husband's touch, knowing instantly that the dwarf was, indeed, her husband.

But Damayanti wondered why he looked so different. So, she took her children and went to visit Bahuka for the first time. As if destiny knew that Bahuka's time was done, Nala transformed back to his original form, and the family was reunited.

Together, they went to Rituparna, and Damayanti apologized for the incorrect message that was sent to him. When the king learnt about Bahuka's true identity, he felt honoured to have received Nala's friendship and honest service.

After some time passed, Nala went back to the kingdom of Nishadha, played another game of dice with his brother, Pushkara, and defeated him, finally winning back his kingdom and living the rest of his days in peace.'

Yudhishthira heaved a deep sigh of relief at the end of the story. He understood what the sage was trying to teach him—that everyone faces their share of challenges in life, and that an individual can conquer these difficulties with patience, courage and intelligence, just like Damayanti had.

Even today, good cooking by a man is often compared to Nala's cooking and is referred to as *nalapaka*. And uttering Damayanti's name brings to mind the visual of Raja Ravi Varma's legendary painting *Hamsa Damayanti*, which portrays Damayanti talking to a golden swan.

The Princess Who Became a Wedding Gift

Battles between gods and demons were a normal occurrence in ancient times.

Brihaspati, the guru of the gods, was renowned for his wisdom. He had an intelligent, handsome and obedient son named Kacha. Meanwhile, the guru of the asuras was Shukracharya, who was extremely sharp, knowledgeable and short-tempered.

Whenever asuras were killed, Shukracharya used a special mantra called the Sanjeevani to bring them back to life. As a result, a time came when asuras began emerging victorious in almost all encounters. No matter how hard or valiantly the devas fought, they inevitably lost because Brihaspati did not possess the knowledge needed for the Sanjeevani mantra.

After consistent and considerable losses, the gods became frustrated and convened a meeting. There, a decision was taken to send Kacha to Shukracharya's ashram with the pretext of serving him but with the underlying mission to learn the life-reviving mantra from him. The gods instructed Kacha, 'Do whatever needs to be done to learn the mantra. The survival of our species depends on it.'

Kacha nodded and set out for his destination.

When he reached Shukracharya's ashram, he bowed to the great master and implored him, 'O sir, I am Kacha, the son of Brihaspati. I have an earnest desire to be your student and serve you. Please accept me as a disciple. I will never give you cause for complaint.'

Guru Shukracharya was a smart man. He understood why Kacha had come to him. But in those days, it was the duty of a teacher to accept a worthy student if he sincerely desired to serve him. Shukracharya thought, 'I can easily accept Kacha as my student. After all, I can teach only what I think is suitable for him.'

True to his word, Kacha served his master very well. Shukracharya taught him many skills but ensured to not teach him the Sanjeevani mantra, being fully aware of the consequences.

Shukracharya had a beautiful daughter called Devayani, who was the apple of his eye. Since her mother's death many years ago, she had developed a close bond with her father, but she often felt lonely.

With the arrival of Kacha, Devayani was happy to have a friend close to her own age. Her father was often busy with his lessons or the matters of the state, and over time, Kacha became a wonderful companion to her. She began telling him everything, including her smallest desires, and Kacha would bring her whatever she wanted. If she yearned for a flower from the forest, Kacha would acquire the exact flower she described. If she wanted to go for a stroll, Kacha would ensure he was there to escort her. Gradually, she fell in love with him.

The asura students who had been keeping an eye on Kacha were unhappy about this turn of events. They suspected the real reason behind Kacha's presence in the ashram but didn't have the courage to discuss it with their teacher.

One day, Shukracharya sent Kacha with instructions to graze the cows. Seizing the opportunity, the asuras murdered Kacha, and the cows returned to the ashram on their own in the evening.

When Kacha did not come back to his teacher's home by nightfall, Devayani became worried about his safety. She went to her father and said softly, 'Father, I am worried about Kacha. He hasn't returned with the cows. Please do something and find him.'

Shukracharya looked up and saw the tears in her eyes. He meditated deeply and learnt about Kacha's miserable fate at the hands of the asuras. Unwilling to disclose to Devayani that their fellow asuras had killed Kacha, he used the Sanjeevani mantra to revive Kacha and ensured his safe return.

A few days later, the asuras made a second attempt to kill Kacha. This time, they threw his body in a well. Secretly, Shukracharya revived Kacha again.

Exasperated, the asuras devised an evil scheme. The next time they killed Kacha, they burnt his body, mixed his ashes with water and filled their guru's drinking pot with this water.

That evening, Shukracharya ate dinner and drank the water from his pot. The evening blended into night and Kacha still did not return. As usual, Devayani sorrowfully requested her father to find him.

After meditating, Shukracharya realized that he would have to tell Devayani the truth. So, he explained what had happened and said, 'My dear daughter, Kacha is now in my stomach, so I cannot revive him.'

A tearful Devayani insisted, 'No, Father, you must bring him back somehow.'

Shukracharya tried to elucidate. 'If I revive Kacha, he will have to come out from my stomach. That means that I must die so that he can live. Tell me, my daughter, do you want your father or your friend? Only one of us can live.'

'I want both of you to be alive and well. Father, you can't make me choose. Please, I love both of you,' asserted Devayani.

'My dear girl, Kacha is no ordinary man. I know the reason behind his request to serve me. The truth is that he wants to learn the Sanjeevani mantra. And if you want both of us to live, the only way is to teach him the mantra while he is in my stomach. After that, I will revive him, but in the process, I will die. Then he must use the mantra to bring me back. But that is a very dangerous move, Devayani. You must understand the consequences of this action. This will destroy the asuras eventually, and it will be unfair to our king. I beseech you—please forget about Kacha.'

But headstrong that she was, Devayani refused to listen to her father. 'I will tell Kacha not to use the mantra for any purpose other than to bring you back to life. He will listen to me. I know he will. Please, bring him back to me.'

His love for his daughter blinded Shukracharya, and he gave in. Just as he had predicted, Kacha emerged from Shukracharya's stomach, killing the guru in the process. Kacha fulfilled his duty and revived his teacher by chanting the mantra until Shukracharya also came back to life.

The place where Shukracharya revealed this precious mantra is in Kopargaon, in the state of Maharashtra. There is also a temple here where people can get married at any time or on any day, without following the usual tradition of identifying the right mahurat, or auspicious time, to get married. Even today, on both sides of the River Godavari, there is a friendly fight between people to showcase the traditional enmity between the two sides— one side dresses up as devas and the other as asuras.

Now Devayani was ecstatic to have both the men in her life safe and sound.

But with this incident, Kacha's mission was complete, and he knew that he had to leave the ashram.

The next day, when Devayani realized that Kacha was about to depart, she was taken aback. 'O Kacha! Why are you leaving?' she asked.

When Kacha did not respond, Devayani started sobbing. 'I love you! I have done everything that I could to keep you alive. You must marry me. Isn't that the right thing to do?'

Kacha smiled gently. 'My dear Devayani, I have always respected you—both as my teacher's daughter and as my friend. I've never had or professed any romantic feelings for you. Now I am born out of your father and have become a brother to you. Please forgive me but I cannot marry you.'

Devayani tried her best to cajole him but failed. Angry and upset, she cursed Kacha. 'The Sanjeevani mantra will never be useful to you because you have used my emotions in an unfair manner to reach your goal. Despite the knowledge you now possess, you will never be able to revive anyone by chanting the mantra.'

The usually calm and collected Kacha became livid and cursed her back. 'O Devayani! You will never marry a sage's son. Your headstrong nature is not suited to the calm and quiet fraternity of the sages. May you marry someone of a clan of that temperament!'

Saying thus, Kacha departed from his teacher's home and Devayani became lonely once more.

Time passed, and one day, Devayani received an invitation to participate in some water games. The invitation was from Sharmishtha, who was her friend and the daughter of the king of the asuras.

Delighted, Devayani went to the specified location on the day of the games. There, she found herself surrounded by the princess's other friends, who were wearing fashionable and expensive clothes. She was the only one in a simple cotton outfit. She realized then that she did not fit in with the rich, princely crowd and how different her world was just because she was the daughter of a sage.

A short while later, everyone entered a water tank, and the girls began splashing around. Princess Sharmishtha took charge and the games began. The group played for hours. Daylight turned to twilight and the games finally came to an end.

The girls stepped out of the water and began changing into dry clothes. Without much light to guide her, Devayani quickly made her way in the dark to the clothes she had brought with her and changed into them.

Just then, Sharmishtha came by in search of her clothes. She looked up and saw her friend Devayani wearing them! Sharmishtha cried out in anger, 'How dare you—the daughter of a poor teacher—have the audacity to wear my

clothes? They are made of silk and gold. You must only wear simple cotton outfits. Give my clothes back to me right now.'

Sharmishtha looked around for Devayani's clothes, found them and threw them at her.

Devayani unrobed and quickly wore her cotton blouse and sari. She felt humiliated and shouted at the princess, 'It was a mistake because of the dark, Sharmishtha! How dare you speak to me this way? My father and his special Sanjeevani mantra are a major reason for the asuras winning the wars against the gods. How can you forget that?'

'Don't talk too much, Devayani. Your father is not doing this out of the goodness of his heart. He is doing it for his livelihood, which is solely dependent on my father. Don't you forget that!' retorted Sharmishtha in disdain.

The argument escalated, and both maidens lost their temper and their minds. The other girls around them witnessed the screaming match from a distance—they didn't know what to do. One was a princess and the other a renowned teacher's dear daughter. Who had the courage to stop them? When it became too dark, the other girls soundlessly went back to their homes.

Meanwhile, in an uncontrollable fit of rage, Sharmishtha pushed Devayani into a waterless well. She was so livid that she left her friend there and headed back to the palace.

As the hours passed, darkness further enveloped Devayani, and it became eerily quiet. She began sobbing. 'I know that my father will find me once he knows that I am missing,' she thought. 'But how long will it be before he starts searching for me? Or perhaps Sharmishtha will lie and say that I am somewhere else. If that happens, I might die here without any food or water.'

She began yelling out in the hope that someone would help her.

Finally, in the wee hours of the morning, a chariot passed in the distance. That chariot belonged to King Yayati, who was the son of Nahusha. He heard a faint cry for help and wondered who it was.

He brought his chariot to a halt and followed the sound of the sobbing girl coming from a well nearby. When he peeped inside, he saw a lone maiden. He couldn't see her face clearly, but due to the early light of the morning, he could faintly see that she was a beautiful girl. He extended his right hand and the maiden placed her right hand in his. With a firm tug, he pulled her out of the well.

Yayati introduced himself. 'I am King Yayati. It is a shock to see a beautiful maiden such as yourself stuck in the well at this hour. What happened?'

Devayani bowed and said, 'I am Devayani, the daughter of Shukracharya, the guru of the asuras. I was intentionally pushed inside the well by a princess. But the important thing is that you have held my right hand and I yours. You must wed me formally now that we have unknowingly completed a ritual usually done during a wedding.'

King Yayati was taken aback. Though Devayani was very beautiful, he knew of her father's reputation and his short temper. 'I have simply helped you, my lady. My intention isn't to get married to you.'

'Neither was mine, but fate has deemed it so, don't you think? It is custom for the daughter of a sage to marry the man who holds her right hand.' She sighed. 'And so, here we are.'

Kacha's curse was coming to fruition.

Yayati agreed, somewhat reluctantly. He was still afraid of what Shukracharya might say or do.

Devayani suggested their next course of action. 'Why don't I go home and talk to my father? You can come to the ashram tomorrow and formally ask for my hand in marriage.'

Back at home, Shukracharya was sick with worry about what had happened to his daughter. 'She should have returned home by nightfall,' he thought. 'She has never been this late before. Has she taken ill? What if something happened to her during the water games? What if she has drowned? How will I live without her? I must do something.'

Disturbed, he began pacing around the house.

Just then, Devayani walked in. Her face was red with anger, and her father could see that she was shaken and upset. Devayani told Shukracharya about everything that had happened. Then she said, 'King Yayati will come tomorrow to ask for my hand in marriage, and I consent to it.'

Shukracharya agreed to the match.

But Devayani's anger flared up again and she said, 'You must ask Sharmishtha's father to make the arrangements for my wedding since you are the most important person in his court. I request you to give me what I ask for when the time comes for you to give me a wedding gift.'

Shukracharya tried to placate her. 'O Devayani! I have helped the king win so many wars that he will give me whatever you desire. Tell me, what would you like as a wedding gift?'

Devayani did not respond.

'Do you want books?' Shukracharya prodded.

'Father, I want neither books nor wealth. My earnest desire is to have Sharmishtha as my slave. She must accompany me to my husband's home.'

Shukracharya was not prepared for such a request. Usually, the daughter of a sage aspired only for knowledge. He tried to convince her to change her mind. 'My dear daughter, I agree that Sharmishtha has made a mistake, but you should forgive her and forget this unpleasant incident. She is the princess of the asuras. You can't order her to be your slave. I promise I will tell her father about her bad behaviour and that she will be punished accordingly. But I will advise you to go to your husband's house in peace and happiness and not take an act of revenge along with you.'

Devayani, however, would not budge. 'Father, I ask for nothing else. This is all that I want.'

Shukracharya knew of his daughter's strong-minded nature. There was nothing he could say that would change her mind. Perhaps her not having grown up with a mother had made him more lenient towards his daughter, resulting in her stubbornness. But now it was too late. He had no option but to approach Sharmishtha's father and the reigning king, Vrishparva.

In the king's court the next morning, Vrishparva was surprised to see Shukracharya, the great guru, approaching him in distress. The king asked him, 'Sir, is everything all right?'

Shukracharya told the king about the incident from the day before and firmly asked him to ensure that Sharmishtha was given as a wedding gift to Devayani.

The king was in a fix. He thought, 'If I don't agree to Shukracharya's demand, then the great guru will definitely walk out of my court. He may even join the gods, which will surely signal my defeat and the end of my reign. No, I can't allow that to happen. Not for the sake of my people. A king must sacrifice for the greater good.'

He sighed. He knew what had to be done. With a heavy heart, the king went to the princess's chamber.

Sharmishtha was unaware of the drama that involved her. She was, in fact, sitting alone near a window and feeling low because she realized that she had treated her friend Devayani unfairly. She cursed herself and her behaviour. 'Why did I have to be so rude to her? She has come to my palace multiple times and has never glanced at or expected fancy jewellery or clothing from me. She is a simple girl who doesn't care for money or display. How will I face Devayani now?'

When she saw her father entering her room and noticed how upset he looked, she thought, 'Guru Shukracharya must have complained to my father about my behaviour. He must be so disappointed in me.'

So, she decided to bring up the topic herself. 'Father! Sometimes my tongue does not cooperate with my mind. I know that I have made a mistake. Please forgive me. I shouldn't have done what I did—not as a princess or as a friend. It is unacceptable. If you want, I will beg forgiveness from Devayani and her father,' she cried.

King Vrishparva sat down and told her what Shukracharya had asked of him.

It was worse than what Sharmishtha could have ever imagined. She wept but eventually agreed with her father's opinion. 'It is true that a princess's life is less precious than her kingdom. I will obey Devayani no matter what it costs me. It probably serves me right,' she said. And so, she agreed to become Devayani's slave.

Thus, Devayani got married to Yayati, and Sharmishtha followed her as a maid to her new home.

Devayani ensured that Sharmishtha was tucked away from the eyes of her husband and the other royal courtiers. Sharmishtha resided in an outhouse at a considerable distance from the main palace, and over time, she was forgotten about and left to her duties.

King Yayati and Devayani did not have an easy marriage. She was stubborn and short-tempered, and the two frequently quarrelled. In time, they had two sons— Yadu and Turvasu.

One day, Yayati was wandering in the royal gardens and saw a beautiful maiden working near an outhouse. He had never seen her before. Something about her graceful movements made him curious. She did not fit the description of a royal maid, despite her clothes. She seemed to be a lady of high rank.

He approached her and asked, 'Who are you?'

Sharmishtha bowed her head, introduced herself and recounted her side of the story. King Yayati took pity on her. He found her to be so attractive, charming and easy to talk to.

After that first meeting, he met her many times and asked her to marry him in secret.

By then, Sharmishtha had also became fond of the king, and despite her reservations, she agreed to marry him. Together, they had three sons—Druhyu, Anu and Puru.

The years passed, and Devayani remained unaware that her husband had also married Sharmishtha.

One day, Devayani's children, Yadu and Turvasu, were playing with a ball a little distance away from the main palace. Suddenly, the ball flew high up in the air and fell near the front door of a small house nearby. Three bright-eyed boys came out and gave the ball back to Yadu.

Devayani had been observing her children from a distance. Even from there, she was drawn to these three boys. She knew they weren't ordinary servants. So, she approached them and asked, 'My dear boys, I have never seen you before. Who are your parents?'

One of the boys replied, 'My mother is Sharmishtha.'

Instantly, Devayani recalled her forgotten friend and slave. 'Who is your father?' she asked.

Just then, Yayati's chariot stopped nearby. The boy pointed at him.

Devayani stood rooted to the spot. 'Does that mean my husband has married my slave and nemesis, Sharmishtha? Would he really do that to me?' she wondered. Her eyes clouded with disgust and anger.

She walked up to her husband. 'Is it true that you are the father of these three boys?' she thundered.

'Yes,' replied Yayati.

Without a word, Devayani turned around and went to her father's home. Once she saw him, she couldn't control her tears and cried her heart out. She told her father about how Yayati had deceived her.

Shukracharya tried to console her. 'Mistakes happen, Devayani. Forget about the past and forgive your husband and Sharmishtha. Be magnanimous and treat the children and their mother well. You are the first wife. The honour and the kingdom will come only to your children.'

But Devayani did not care. She wanted to punish Yayati and begged her father, 'I want you to curse my dishonest husband.'

'Think about the consequences to your children, Devayani,' Shukracharya advised.

She continued as if she hadn't heard him. 'Curse him so that he loses his youthful good looks and body, and instead, becomes an old man immediately. Then he won't be able to attract any women.'

Once again, his love for his daughter overwhelmed Shukracharya, and he used his yogic powers to curse his son-in-law.

When Yayati learnt of the curse he was to face, he came and fell at Shukracharya's feet and asked for forgiveness.

Shukracharya felt sorry about the price Yayati would have to pay for his mistake, so, with kindness, he modified the curse. 'May you turn old immediately, but if some young man is willing to exchange his youth for your old age, you can become young again. At a time that you deem appropriate, you will have to reverse this and give the man back his youth and accept your old age.'

King Yayati bowed, thankful for the leeway that he had been given. 'I want to be young for a little while longer and enjoy whatever life has to offer,' he thought.

He left Shukracharya's house with the hope that one of his sons from Devayani would be ready to temporarily give their youth to him. To his dismay, both Yadu and Turvasu declined to do so.

Yayati became upset with the two boys. 'I raised you thinking that you would be my successors when the time comes, but you are not ready to sacrifice even a little for your father's sake. I promise you this—neither you nor your lineage will ever rule a kingdom.'

Today, it is a well-known fact that Yadu's lineage, the Yadavas, never ruled a kingdom. Lord Krishna was born in the same dynasty but never sat on the throne. Aware of his ancestral history and despite his eligibility to be king, Krishna chose to crown his grandfather Ugrasen instead.

Disappointed with Yadu and Turvasu, Yayati approached the sons he had with Sharmishtha. Puru looked to his mother for guidance.

Sharmishtha said quietly, 'It is the duty of a son to help his father.'

Puru understood and offered his father his young body. Immediately, Yayati became young again, while Puru aged and became an old man.

For many, many years, Yayati lived happily and enjoyed his youth. Much later, he realized the fruitlessness of the human body and exchanged it back with Puru. Puru and his successors eventually became the emperors of the dynasty. The lineage of Puru then became known as the Kurus, who ruled Hastinapur and became the originators of the great epic Mahabharata.

Two Stars of True Love

Arundhati was the eighth among the nine daughters of Sage Kardama, the son of Brahma, and his wife, Devahuti. She was the grandmother of Sage Parashara and the great-grandmother of the sage Veda Vyasa, the author of the Mahabharata.

As a young girl, Arundhati was inclined towards learning and intellectual debates. When she grew up, she married Vasishtha, one of the famous seven sages, or Saptarishis.

Indian astronomy identifies these seven sages as seven stars, while the West relates to them as the stars in the Ursa Major constellation. Arundhati is also often considered to represent a star named Alcor, and its companion, Mizar, represents Vasishtha.

After marriage, Arundhati continued her lessons. She would finish her chores as soon as she could and join her husband's class to learn what Vasishtha taught his students. Vasishtha was a prodigious exponent of the three Vedas: Yajur Veda, Sama Veda and Rig Veda. Many students vied to attend his classes in the gurukul.

One day, Vasishtha was talking to his students about dharma. Suddenly, Arundhati asked him, 'If you don't mind, may I take over from you today and teach the class this lesson?'

Vasishtha was surprised at his wife's unusual request, but he agreed. To his pleasant surprise, Arundhati explained the concept of dharma very clearly to his students.

After the class, Vasishtha said to her, 'You really are my partner and my equal half. You have understood my teachings and my mind. From now on, help me with my classes.'

When Brahma learnt of this development, he was pleased and sent the magical cow Nandini to Vasishtha's ashram so that she could help Arundhati with her chores. This way, Arundhati would be able to devote more time to the pursuit and teaching of knowledge.

One day, Vishvamitra, who was then a king, went hunting with his troop. After the hunt, he felt very thirsty but could not find water anywhere. As the group walked farther into the woods, they came across Vasishtha's ashram.

Vishvamitra instructed a few of his soldiers, 'The hermit lives deep in the forest and may not have many rations. Besides, we are far too many in number. So, please request him politely and ask whether he can spare a little water for us.'

The soldiers went inside the ashram and informed Sage Vasishtha about the king's request.

Vasishtha and Arundhati immediately came out to meet the king and invite him in. Vasishtha said, 'Welcome, dear king, to our small sanctuary. Please relax inside. We will provide whatever you and your troop needs.'

Within a few minutes, Vasishtha had arranged for good food, fruits and water for the king's group.

The king said, 'I really appreciate the trouble you are taking for us. But first, I would love to take a bath if there is enough water available. I wish I had another pair of clothes since the ones I am wearing are dirty now.'

'Please don't worry,' said Vasishtha. 'Everything will be ready for you.'

After his bath, the king was given robes befitting his royal status, and the group was served a sumptuous meal.

The king was curious. 'O Vasishtha, how did you arrange so much—from a royal feast to my wonderful clothes—in such little time?'

'Lord Brahma has been very kind to us and sent Nandini to our ashram to help take care of our guests and chores,' replied Arundhati, pointing to the wish-fulfilling cow who was standing in the garden in front of them. 'There she is! She gave us whatever you desired.'

Vishvamitra was fascinated. 'What a powerful cow!' he thought. 'But Vasishtha is only an ordinary sage. He is underutilizing Nandini by asking her only for food and clothes. If she were with me, I would work towards expanding the kingdom, killing my enemies and taking care of the welfare of my soldiers and subjects.'

Bringing his attention back to Arundhati and Vasishtha, he said, 'O dear sage! I think that I need Nandini much more than you do. Please part with her and give her to me. In return, I will give you whatever you ask for, whether it be hundreds of acres of land, thousands of cows or heaps of gold and silver. I really need Nandini to be with me.'

Vasishtha smiled and said, 'I do not own Nandini. She has her own mind and personality. She has come to us

from Brahma on the condition that we use her only for the good of others and not for ourselves or our personal desires. She is a big boon to us because Arundhati and I are both busy with our teaching, and we cannot manage without her. I apologize sincerely, but I cannot give her to you.'

The king was upset. 'I will teach this sage a lesson,' he thought. He instructed his soldiers, 'Bring Nandini to me right now. Use force if the situation demands it. We are taking her back to the capital city.'

When Nandini heard this, she became distraught. Then she turned towards Vishvamitra and gazed at him intently. Suddenly, thousands of warriors emerged from her horns and began killing the king's soldiers. Within minutes, all the king's soldiers were dead.

Vishvamitra became ashamed at his unpardonable behaviour. He realized that Vasishtha was a much better man than him because of his knowledge and calm demeanour. The king thought, 'What is the use of all my power and strength when Vasishtha is stronger than me without even owning an army?'

So, he turned to Vasishtha and said, 'From this day on, I will not work towards the expansion of my kingdom or the collection of wealth. I will pursue knowledge—the most powerful possession of them all!'

Saying thus, Vishvamitra gave up everything, including his right to the throne. In time, he became a great and knowledgeable sage. However, he was always competitive with Vasishtha and never attained the supreme knowledge or the spirit of compassion befitting a true sage.

Vishvamitra yearned for Vasishtha to acknowledge him as a Brahmarishi, the highest title for a sage next to Saptarishi. However, Vasishtha would not. This encouraged Vishvamitra to trouble Vasishtha's students. Still, Vasishtha would not budge.

One day, Vishvamitra came to Vasishtha's ashram at night in order to spy on him. This way, he could obtain an understanding of Vasishtha's study matter and then work towards surpassing him. Unexpectedly, he overheard a conversation between Vasishtha and Arundhati.

'Poor Vishvamitra has done so much penance,' said Arundhati, 'but he still hasn't reached the highest level possible for a sage. Why is that so?'

'I really care for him and love him, Arundhati. But I don't acknowledge it for his own good. The moment I do, he will not pursue knowledge any more. He needs to go on. The ultimate quality of a sage is compassion. Right now, he thinks that knowledge brings power, but the truth is that it is knowledge with compassion that brings the supreme power that is helpful to mankind.'

Hearing this, Vishvamitra felt mortified and realized the depth of Vasishtha's words. He left the ashram and decided to keep pursuing knowledge.

After spending a lot of time with Arundhati and Vasishtha, Nandini went back to Brahmaloka, the abode of Brahma. Meanwhile, Vasishtha and his students decided to go to the Himalayas for penance, and Arundhati stayed back in the ashram with the remaining students until they returned.

While Vasishtha and his students were away, a great famine fell upon the kingdom.

Vasishtha found out about this through his yogic powers and prayed to Shiva, 'Lord, please protect my wife as she fights through this alone in the ashram.'

Arundhati, on the other hand, prayed, 'O Shiva, please protect my husband. I am on land and may survive, but I wonder about the state of my poor husband. I pray that he returns soon after the penance.'

Within a few days, the gurukul was also shut down due to the famine in the area. Arundhati continued to live alone in the ashram.

One day, a young boy appeared in front of the ashram gates and said to Arundhati, 'O Mother, I am famished. Can you tell me where Sage Vasishtha's ashram is? I heard that it is nearby.'

'My dear child,' said Arundhati, 'this is his ashram, but he is away and will be gone for a while since he is performing a penance for the welfare of the land and the people. What do you need?'

'I have come from far away—from the Himalayas. I don't have parents, and I have nowhere to go. I came here in the hope of learning the Vedas from the sage. But alas! He is not here. What will I do now?'

'Please stay here then. There is a famine, but I will share whatever I have. I can also teach you, if you allow me. It may be some time before the sage returns, but don't you worry. We can manage until then.' Arundhati gave him some roasted seeds to eat and apologized for the lack of rice.

Thus, the boy settled down at the ashram and took lessons from her every day.

As the days passed, Arundhati taught the boy the Vedas and continued to pray for the safe return of her husband and his students.

At last, Vasishtha came back with his disciples. He was happy to see his wife in good spirits. 'O Arundhati, Shiva has heard my prayers. He has looked after you well!'

'Husband, I am also ecstatic that you have returned safely. The lord has heard my prayers too!'

Vasishtha spotted the little boy. He asked his wife, 'Who is this?'

Just as Arundhati finished telling the sage about the boy's arrival and his circumstances, the boy manifested into Lord Shiva himself! He had heard both their prayers indeed. He smiled at Arundhati. 'I am fortunate to have learnt the Vedas from you. Your affection and devotion for Vasishtha cannot be measured by any mortal standards. In time, you will become a star in the sky, along with your husband. You will be an eternal example for humans everywhere, and every married couple will look up to you.'

Shiva turned to Vasishtha. 'Arundhati is your true partner! May the gods bless both of you.'

Saying thus, Shiva disappeared.

In the culture of some homes today, a newly-wed bride and groom are shown the stars of Arundhati and Vasishtha at night so that they can be inspired to be like the couple. Even very old couples are sometimes referred to as Vasishtha–Arundhati in order to respect their love and commitment to each other.

Today, Arundhati has become a name synonymous with chastity, devotion and happiness associated with marriage, and plays about her are often showcased all over the country.

The Curse of Immortality

A long time ago, two sages named Nara and Narayana were performing a penance for the welfare of the people on earth. Their penance was intense, and they lived in the Badrika ashram in the Himalayas.

When the king of the gods, Indra, learnt of this development from his spies, he became worried and even more insecure than usual. What if the sages asked for Indra's throne as the fruit of their penance? So, he came up with a wicked plan to disturb them.

Indra's court boasted exquisite dancers, or apsaras, such as Rambha, Tilottama, Pushpalata and Menaka. He called Rambha and Pushpalata and instructed them, 'Your task is to spoil the penance of the two meditating sages Nara and Narayana. I will send Manmatha, the god of love, to help hasten the process.'

The apsaras nodded and descended down to the earth. There, Manmatha created a stunning ambience of springtime around the two sages. The blooming flowers and their sweet scent, fresh green trees, beautiful ponds and chirping birds made it an enchanting place for romance. Still, the sages did not open their eyes.

Manmatha said to the apsaras, 'I have done my duty. I refuse to stand here like the last time I did with Shiva only to end up in ashes. Now, the job is all yours.'

Soon, the god of love left.

Rambha and Pushpalata began to dance and sing, but it was of no use—Nara and Narayana continued to meditate.

Afraid of displeasing Indra, they approached Narayana and touched him. They said, 'O sage, you don't need this penance to reach the heavens. We are here, and this place around you is itself heaven. Open your eyes.'

Narayana, now disturbed, opened his eyes. He became furious as he glanced around him and understood what was happening. 'How dare you come here without our permission and create an environment we are least interested in?'

Rambha and Pushpalata grew deathly pale as even Nara opened his eyes. They were aware that accomplished sages could give powerful curses with the potential to alter the course of their lives. Immediately, the two dancers fell at Narayana's feet and pleaded with him. 'Forgive us. We did not intend to cause you any harm, and yet, we are bound by the laws of our realm. Our master, Indra, ordered us to do his bidding, and we must fulfil our duty to him. Please, have mercy on us.'

Narayana was upset with Indra. He said to the apsaras, 'I understand your position, but I cannot forgive Indra. He is a coward who uses his dancers as a weapon.'

Indra, who was watching from the heavens, became afraid that the sage was just about to curse him. He had always gambled by sending beautiful apsaras to distract people from their focused penance. Sometimes the plan would

work, such as in the case of Vishvamitra, but sometimes it boomeranged, like now.

In a flash, Indra appeared in front of Nara and Narayana. 'Sorry, my dear sages,' he said and folded his hands. 'Please forgive me!'

'I was performing a penance for the benefit of the people on earth,' said Narayana, 'but you always assume that any meditating sage is greedy for your throne. The truth is that most of us couldn't care less about immortality or your throne. You send these helpless women to attract us. They may be the most stunning beings in the heavens, but with my powers, I can create a better and more gorgeous woman than all these apsaras.'

Saying thus, Narayana created a striking maiden. Indeed, her beauty was unearthly and the kind that the world had never seen. When she came and touched his feet, Narayana turned to Indra and said, 'This is Urvashi, my mortal daughter from the penance. Just look at her—she is the most beautiful maiden in the world and is filled with good virtues. You will not find anyone like her.'

Instantly, Indra felt that his wife, Shachi, and all the other apsaras paled in comparison to Urvashi's beauty. He bowed down to the sage and said, 'If you allow it, may I take her to my abode? I will make her the head of the apsaras.'

Narayana smiled. 'I am a sage, and I don't need my daughter's company for penance. If she is willing, you may take her with you.'

With Urvashi's consent, Indra took her to heaven.

Heavy discussions began in Indra's court.

Only the immortal could stay in the heavens. How could a human be allowed to enter the realm in her mortal body? No, she could enter only after she'd died and lost her human form.

The debate went on until the gods finally saw Urvashi. Once they did, they immediately agreed to give her citizenship in their realm, which blessed her with all the qualities of a god: immortality, the power to transform, the ability to travel in an instant and many others. Though Urvashi was of human origin, she could live in the heavens forever.

At first, Urvashi was hesitant. She had the power of the gods, but her heart remained human. She yearned for genuine company and requested Indra to allow her to have a pet.

Indra laughed and said, 'You don't need my permission for that! Every god has a vehicle that is in the form of an animal. I have the elephant Airavata, Shiva has the bull Nandi and Vishnu has the bird Garuda.'

Urvashi decided that she would like to keep a sheep. The animal was so soft and sweet that she became a constant part of Urvashi's life.

Meanwhile, Bharata Muni, the father of Indian classical dance, saw Urvashi's outstanding dancing skills and requested Indra, 'I have written a play known as *Lakshmi Swayamvara*. I have been searching for a suitable maiden to play the lead role for a long time, and I have found what I have been looking for in Urvashi—she resembles Lakshmi in her appearance and in her virtues. I can't think of anyone else to play this role. Will you please allow her to do so?'

'Of course! Please go ahead,' said Indra and gave his blessing.

Urvashi was thrilled when she found out that she was getting the opportunity to play the main character in a famous sage's play!

Unknown to Urvashi, there lived an asura named Kesi, the current king of the asuras. One day, his spies told him about Urvashi and her magnificence. Immediately, Kesi wanted to kidnap her because he thought he deserved a beautiful wife such as her.

While he was discussing the plan of abduction, the wandering sage Narada came by and heard what was going on. He laughed and said, 'Kesi, I think you should drop your plans. Urvashi lives in the heavens, and Indra has many mighty and helpful human friends. For instance, the Chandravamshi king Pururava is a great warrior and a friend of the gods. You will only start a great war if you kidnap Urvashi. Use good strategy instead. Sometimes, these apsaras get bored of the scenery and the ease of heaven. After all, they are immortal and have been seeing the same things forever. So, they come down here to enjoy the earth's beauty, which is unavailable in the realm above. They enjoy the natural variation of the different seasons and the taste of food that changes as mankind evolves and experiments. Use that chance to meet Urvashi and profess your love for her. Genuine love will attract any woman.'

Narada's words made sense, and Kesi was convinced. He decided to wait for an appropriate time to see Urvashi.

Soon, Bharata Muni decided to stage the play *Lakshmi Swayamvara* at Kubera's court. Kubera, the god of wealth, sent his vehicle Pushpaka Vimana to escort the actors to the court.

On the way, Urvashi and her friends looked down at the earth and saw that it was the rainy season. Misty clouds floated in the sky, and the planet looked lush and verdant. Urvashi became homesick and suggested, 'Come, let's take a break and stop for a while. We can enjoy the green beauty of the earth.'

Everyone agreed.

The Pushpaka Vimana was brought to a halt at the top of a hill. Everyone stepped down and enjoyed the surroundings.

Kesi took this chance to see Urvashi. She was so beautiful that he knew she would not accept him. So, he returned to his previous plan of kidnapping and marrying her. He transformed himself into a whirlwind and snatched Urvashi away from her friends, who began screaming for help. King Pururava, who was passing by, heard the cries and followed Kesi. Soon, a fierce fight took place between them, and Kesi lost.

After the battle, Pururava looked at Urvashi clearly for the first time and fell in love with her too. She was unimaginably exquisite. To her surprise, Urvashi also returned his feelings, despite her having seen many gods and humans in her life. With a heavy heart, the two went their separate ways—Urvashi to Kubera's court in the Pushpaka Vimana and Pururava back to his kingdom.

However, day and night, Urvashi thought of Pururava and fell short at perfecting her rehearsal. Everybody thought it was a passing phase, as apsaras never fell in love with any one person so deeply. But Urvashi's heart was human, and the other apsaras did not understand her feelings.

On the day of the performance, the court was overcrowded with people excited to see the show. Even Vishnu and Lakshmi were present. The play began with great pomp.

When Urvashi stood up to garland Vishnu during the climax of the show, she was supposed to say, 'Of all the beings in the world—sura, asura and others—I garland Vishnu.' However, Urvashi, who was immersed in thoughts of Pururava, said, 'I garland Pururava.'

Everyone was astounded, and silence filled the room.

The play was brought to a halt, and Bharata Muni became upset. He said, 'I have persevered and taken years to find a perfect lead. Even Lakshmi and Vishnu are here, looking at a genuine and true depiction of their life. But you have spoilt it completely by uttering the name of a human. I curse you—may you lose citizenship of the heavens and become human, only to live on the earth. You don't deserve to live elsewhere.'

Within seconds, Urvashi found herself on earth as a mortal along with her sheep.

Little did she know that this curse had created havoc in the heavens. Indra was greatly distressed but did not have the courage to do anything heroic to reverse the curse. The greatest gem of his court had been snatched away due to a small error. He went and pleaded with Bharata Muni to forgive Urvashi. The sage said, 'Fine, here is the solution. Whenever Urvashi becomes pregnant and her husband learns of the baby, she will cease to become human and revert to your realm—she will be exactly as she was before.'

Neither Indra nor Bharata Muni paid attention to what Urvashi desired. They simply assumed that everyone, including her, would be happy to be immortal and live in the heavens.

Unaware of the modification of the curse and the fact that her time on earth was temporary, Urvashi was happy to find herself in this situation. She was thrilled to be a mortal. Now back with Pururava, she was happy. Deeply in love, they got married and quickly became inseparable.

When Indra learnt of Urvashi's blissful relationship with Pururava, he became unhappy and jealous. His spies decided to take some action, and without telling him, they stole Urvashi's sheep at night.

When Urvashi couldn't find her sheep the next morning, she decided to search for it herself. During her quest, she entered a jungle that belonged to Karthikeyan, the son of Shiva. She did not know that the jungle carried a special rule—no woman was allowed to enter. Once she went in, she wasn't allowed to leave and became a prisoner. When she requested Karthikeyan's soldiers for a meeting with him, they refused her earnest requests again and again until she gave up.

Meanwhile, Pururava had begun an aggressive search for his wife on his own. At last, a messenger came and informed him about Urvashi's arrest in Karthikeyan's jungle. Quickly, Pururava departed for the forest to meet Karthikeyan and requested him to release his wife. Kind Karthikeyan, who knew of Pururava and his strength, agreed and allowed Urvashi to leave.

As soon as Indra learnt of Urvashi's release, he realized that Pururava's love for his wife ran deep and that he was capable of combatting even Karthikeyan, the commander-in-chief of the gods' army. So, his best course of action was to send the sheep back as if it had just wandered off, and he instructed his soldiers to do so.

Soon, the couple went back to their happy life. After some time, Urvashi found out that she was pregnant. She was ecstatic and waited impatiently to share this news with her husband. But before she could, her friend Rambha came down from the heavens, took her aside and told her about how the curse had been modified. 'Urvashi, please don't tell Pururava about this development. If you do, you will have to leave him right after that. If you really love him and want to be with him, don't let him know about the baby,' she said.

Urvashi was shattered. She sobbed, 'Why can't I have a normal family with a husband and a child? Now I must choose between two impossible options: If I want to be with my husband, then I have to leave my child; and if I choose my child, I have to abandon my husband.'

No matter how much she tried, Urvashi couldn't find a way to be with both her husband and her child. Others had made a decision about her life, and she had no power to change these circumstances.

After days of worry and thought, she formulated a plan. She knew that Sage Chyavana and his wife, Sukanya, were a good and pious couple who lived in the forest nearby.

When she sensed that the time was right, Urvashi said to her husband, 'I want to spend some time with Sage Chyavana and Sukanya. A few months would be nice.'

'Of course, my dear. Shall we go together?'

'No, I want to do this alone, husband. That is my greatest desire. Besides, you must continue to rule the kingdom and take care of your subjects.'

Pururava was not a headstrong husband, so he agreed to his wife's wishes. He only wanted to see her happy.

Urvashi went to Sage Chyavana and Sukanya and explained her strange situation to them. They were kind and looked after her until she had her baby boy, whom she named Ayur. With sadness in her eyes, she gave the baby to the couple and said, 'From this day on, this child is yours. Please take care of him as your own and ensure that he is raised to be a good man. He is born a prince, so I will be grateful if you could also teach him archery. I don't know when these circumstances will change so that I can come back for him. Right now, my first duty is towards my husband.'

With a heavy heart and tears spilling from her eyes, Urvashi left the ashram and returned to Pururava, who remained unaware of the birth of his son.

Ten years passed, and Urvashi often thought of her child.

In the heavens, Indra grew impatient and upset at Urvashi's absence. He had assumed that she would have returned to his court by now. He thought to himself, 'I can see how Urvashi is sacrificing a big part of her life to be with Pururava. There will be no end to this. I must trick them so that she will come back here quickly.'

He called two of his spies and instructed one of them, 'Urvashi wears a special necklace. Her husband has given it to her, and it is a precious family heirloom with immense sentimental value. The next time she is out with her husband

and in the vicinity of Chyavana's ashram, you transform into a vulture and grab the necklace from her. Then you fly as high as you possibly can. I will take care of the rest.'

Indra turned to the second spy and said, 'Dress like a poor sage and go to Chyavana's ashram. Distract Ayur and make him somehow spot the vulture. The rest will automatically fall into place.'

Just as Indra had schemed, the magical vulture seized Urvashi's necklace while she was out on a stroll with her husband and flew high into the sky before anyone could react.

At the same time, a poor sage entered Chyavana's ashram. He saw Ayur practising with his bow and arrow and began speaking to him. 'Can you shoot very far?' he asked. 'I don't think a ten-year-old can shoot at a very long distance.'

'I can do much more than that,' replied Ayur with the confidence only a young boy can have.

'Really?'

Ayur nodded.

'Well, see that vulture in the sky? He is carrying something. If you are as good as you say you are, can you bring the vulture to the ground and give me what he has?'

'That is very easy,' said the young boy and aimed his next arrow at the vulture.

Meanwhile, Pururava had been on horseback, keenly tracking the movements of the vulture in order to shoot him down. Urvashi was following him but had been left far behind. 'How dare that bird snatch the heirloom from my wife's neck?' he thought. He took aim and shot an arrow at the vulture.

Just as Indra had planned, two arrows were shot from two bows at the same time. Both the arrows touched the vulture, who released the necklace from his grip and disappeared.

Both Pururava and the boy ran to the spot in which the necklace fell. Ayur reached first and picked up the necklace. He had never seen such sparkling gold! Fascinated, he wondered what it was. Just then, Pururava also came along and saw the necklace in Ayur's hand. The king said, 'O little boy! I shot the vulture first. Give me the necklace; it belongs to me.'

'No, I shot the arrow first. I even reached here and saw the necklace first. I will give this to Guru Ma. This will make her day,' said the bright boy.

'Dear boy, I think you have failed to recognize me. I am Pururava, the mighty king and the great archer. I don't miss whatever I decide to target—'

'I am very good at archery too,' interrupted the young boy. 'I don't miss my shot either.'

Pururava tried to reason with him. 'But you are a hermit. What is the use of this necklace to you? It belongs to my family. If you would like, I can give you land and many cows.'

'But I don't want those things. I want this necklace.'

Patiently, Pururava continued to request him, but Ayur refused to listen.

'Listen, boy. You are forcing me to take a stand. Why don't I show you my archery skills?' said the king, pointing an arrow at Ayur.

Ayur glared at the king and said, 'Why don't I show you mine too?' He aimed an arrow back at Pururava.

By then, Sukanya and Urvashi also reached the spot.

'Stop it, Ayur!'

'Stop, Pururava!'

The moment Urvashi saw Sukanya, she understood who the boy was and couldn't resist smiling.

Sukanya decided that it was time. She had to unveil the truth. 'The two of you cannot fight each other,' she said. 'It is forbidden.'

'Why?' asked Pururava.

'Because he is your son, my king,' said Sukanya in a faint voice.

'What do you mean? You must be mistaken.'

Urvashi answered her husband's query. 'Ten years ago, I came here and gave birth to your son because I was made aware of a change in the curse that Bharata Muni had put on me. Later Indra had asked for the curse to be modified with this condition: If you ever learnt that we have a child together, then I would have to return to Indra's court. I knew that you couldn't live without me, and so, I hid the birth of Ayur from you.'

'O Urvashi, what a sacrifice you have made for me! Had you told me, I would have fought my hardest against Indra—' said Pururava.

But before he could even finish the sentence, Urvashi disappeared from sight. She had returned to Indra's abode. It was a bittersweet moment for Pururava. With tears in his eyes, he embraced his son, Ayur. Together, the father and son bade farewell to Chyavana and Sukanya, and they went back to the capital without Urvashi.

In his palace, Pururava thought about his wife night and day. His life was hard without her. He loved his son, but nobody could fill Urvashi's place in his heart. In Indra's court, Urvashi was extremely unhappy and constantly thought of her family.

One day, Pururava thought, 'I have helped Indra in many wars and brought victory to him. Still, he has been unfair to my wife. I cannot take it anymore. I must wage a war against him to get my wife back. My family is suffering because of him.'

Convinced that this was the right thing to do, Pururava ordered his soldiers to prepare for war.

When Indra heard of this, he strongly felt that he would not win against Pururava. Besides, he would lose a valuable ally too. The best way to defuse the situation was to send Urvashi back to earth. He would lose his gem, but her heart was human and she was filled with pure love for her family. It was better to let her go. So, Indra took Urvashi to Pururava and said, 'I am amazed at the love between you and your wife. Here she is. With her determination, she managed to hide Ayur and her maternal feelings for a long time. I bless her. She will continue to retain her citizenship in the heavens and can use the powers of an apsara when she chooses to.'

Pururava thanked Indra and the gods for their blessings and felt grateful to have a devoted wife and a bright son.

There is a popular play written by Kalidasa based on this story called *Vikramōrvaśīyam*.

The First Clone in the World

Sanjana was the beautiful daughter of Vishwakarma, the great engineer and architect of the heavens. He wanted Sanjana to marry a powerful god, and advised her. 'There are only three suitable contenders for you,' Vishwakarma told his daughter, 'three who can generate light in your life: Vidyut, the god of lightning; Agni, the god of fire; and Surya, the sun god. Whom would you like to marry, dear daughter?'

Sanjana thought for a while and said, 'Lightning is temporary. It only comes at night along with rain and thunder. Even fire arrives only when it is intentionally lit. The sun, however, holds a constant presence in the world and is helpful to mankind. So, Surya is the most powerful of them all. I would like to marry him.'

An alliance was made, and soon, the two were happily wed.

When Sanjana went to live with Surya after the wedding, she realized that he was everything she had ever desired in a husband. But she hadn't accounted for one thing—the immense heat he emanated. Surya's intensity was so fierce that Sanjana found it very difficult to live with him.

Finally, she made an excuse so that she could visit her father to talk about this problem. When she explained the situation to him, Vishwakarma used his expertise to reduce the sun's energy. With the unused energy, brightness and dust, Vishwakarma created three divine objects.

The first object was the Pushpaka Vimana, the vehicle that could traverse all the realms. It was given to Kubera, the god of wealth. However, Ravana, the lord of Lanka, snatched it away from Kubera and later used it to kidnap Sita. After Ravana's death, the vehicle was inherited by his brother Vibhishana.

The second object was the *trishula*, or trident, for Shiva. The god of destruction would hand over the trident to his wife, Parvati, when needed, who used the weapon to kill asuras. The rest of the time, Shiva kept it with himself. Today, the trident is synonymous with Shiva and his presence.

The last object was the discus, the Sudarshana Chakra, which was given to Vishnu, the god of preservation. The god is almost always represented holding the discus in his hand. Mythology describes the chakra as a weapon that has 108 sharp edges in two rows that move in a circular manner and in opposite directions. It is found across stories in Hindu mythology: Vishnu used it to behead Rahu and Ketu, the two asuras pretending to be gods so that they could obtain the nectar of immortality. It was also used to cut the mountain of Mandara in order to convert it into a churning rod to be used for the churning of the ocean. The discus was also used by Krishna, one of Vishnu's ten avatars, on rare occasions in the Mahabharata. The first time, Krishna used it to behead Shishupala, who insulted him during a yagna, and the second time, he used it to create the illusion of a sunset in order to facilitate the slaying of the enemy Jayadhrata. During its last use, Krishna wielded it to display his true form to the warrior Bhishma and to encourage Arjuna to fight the great war with his full potential.

Once Vishwakarma finished creating the divine objects, Sanjana went back to her marital home with hope in her heart. This time, Sanjana felt an obvious reduction in Surya's energy. However, she still could not bear it. If she went to her father's home again, Surya would call her back in some time, and her father too would send her back, asking her to talk it out with her husband. Sanjana thought hard. She was the daughter of a creative engineer and had learnt a few tricks from her father over the years. So, she decided to clone herself but with one tweak—her clone would easily be able to withstand the sun's warmth. She named her clone Chaya and instructed her to behave exactly like her and to live with Surya.

> Sanjana is credited as the first person in Hindu mythology
> to have thought of and carried out the concept of cloning.

After she created the clone, Sanjana went to her father's home to relax and spend some time with him, at ease with the knowledge that Surya wouldn't call her back. She decided she would return when she was ready.

In the sun god's home, Surya wasn't able to distinguish between Chaya and Sanjana, and Chaya continued to stay with him. In time, she gave birth to a son and named him Shani. When news of the birth reached Vishwakarma's abode, he was furious and confronted his daughter. Left with

no other choice, Sanjana admitted to her scheme and told him about the clone.

Vishwakarma was aghast. 'My dear child, you have done a terrible wrong. Cloning disturbs the balance of nature and the equilibrium of the human race. Don't ever do that again. Now go back to your husband's home.'

Realizing her folly, Sanjana returned to her marital home. She destroyed the clone and somehow managed to live with her husband, despite the terrible heat. Shani didn't realize that his mother was no more and kept thinking of Sanjana as his mother. Time passed, and Sanjana gave birth to twins, Yama and Yami—a boy and a girl.

Now Surya had three children, including Shani. But Shani constantly reminded Sanjana of Chaya, and she gradually became resentful towards him. She neglected him, and over time, the poor boy began getting depressed. He had no idea that Sanjana was not his real mother. He often wondered why she would single him out. Surya, on the other hand, was too busy with his godly duties to realize that his son was upset and frustrated. Sometimes, when Shani became lazy, Sanjana would exaggerate his behaviour when talking to her husband. Gradually, this created a rift between father and son.

When the children became young adults, Surya called them to his chambers and said, 'You are all old enough to handle more duties, and I have decided to give each of you some responsibility.'

To Yami, he said, 'You are a wonderful daughter. Go and flow on the earth as the River Yamuna. You will be lucky because Lord Vishnu, in the form of Krishna, will grow up around you for a period of time. People who take a dip in your waters will wash away their sins, and the women who take a bath in you during the festival of Diwali and pray for their siblings will see all their wishes come true. You will be represented in temples as a lady with a tortoise because of the number of tortoises that will reside in your waters.'

Yami accepted her responsibility gladly and departed for earth.

Then Surya turned to Yama. 'You will be placed in charge of the protection of Dharma, the deity of justice. You will rule the world in a fair manner. You will keep a count of every being's good karma and bad karma, and at their death, you will dole out punishment and reward accordingly. You will uphold your duty to every human sincerely, without mercy or favour. May you be blessed with knowledge. From this day on, you will be called Yamadharma.'

Yamadharma also accepted his responsibility gladly and departed for Mrityuloka, the place where all souls go after death.

Now, Surya turned to Shani and said, 'You are completely useless. I will not give you any responsibility.'

Shani was taken aback. He had not expected this treatment from his own father. He looked at Sanjana. 'Mother? Why are you quiet? Be honest with me—you haven't cared for me since I was young. Whenever I fight with Father, you don't try to stop it. Because of your behaviour, I have become a frustrated and depressed man. What kind of parent are you? Nobody should have a mother like you—'

Sanjana was livid. She interrupted him, 'You have abused your mother. A mother is the strongest force in this world, no matter how she is. I curse that your legs get paralyzed from this moment on.'

Immediately, Shani fell to the ground, as one of his legs gave way and showed signs of paralysis.

Surya was startled by Sanjana's ferocity. 'Shani's behaviour is understandable. He is young and still learning the ways of the world. But how can a mother curse her child?' he wondered.

He turned to Sanjana and said, 'I am astounded by the harsh and quick curse you have placed upon your own son. How can you do this? It is your duty to console him and guide him with patience. I am beginning to think that there is some truth to Shani's allegations. Tell me—what is going on?'

Sanjana, who had been holding this secret in her heart for a long time, couldn't contain it any longer and spilled the beans about Chaya and her son, Shani.

Surya's heart filled with compassion for the motherless boy. He said, 'My son, I have made a grave mistake. I am guilty of being too busy with my duties to notice the difference between Sanjana and Chaya. But that is no excuse. The fact is that you have suffered dearly because of my error. I will reverse Sanjana's curse, but a small limp will always remain in your leg because I, too, don't have the power to neutralize a mother's curse completely. Now, try and stand.'

As Shani stood up, Surya added, 'I have given your brother the grave responsibility of judgement after death, and you, my son, I give the harder responsibility of doling out judgements, punishments and rewards, but it will be during people's lifetimes so they can learn and improve themselves. You will have an indispensable place in the planetary system as Saturn. Do your duty sincerely, without favour or fear, just like your brother, Yama. You will have control over people's egos and will check their nature, leading them to prosperity. You will not spare anyone from the consequence of their actions, irrespective of whether they are a human, god or demon. I am sorry that I can't undo the past or take away your suffering. But I assure you that this position will make you the most powerful planet.'

Shani was surprised. 'I am happy that the truth has been disclosed,' he said. 'Now, I can find closure and peace in this revelation. Father, I will obey your orders. I will appear in every person's life a maximum of three times, and each time, I will stay with him or her for seven-and-a-half years. It will be called Sade Sati. The person will feel pain as intense as my suffering, but they will emerge stronger and purer from the experience, and I will be very compassionate with him or her. Since we both have a history of conflict, I will not stay with you in the same house in an astrological horoscope to avoid further difficulties.'

Surya nodded in agreement and Shani departed.

Surya now turned his focus towards his wife. He was furious with Sanjana, and so, he increased the intensity of his heat until she was forced to leave her home and her husband. Sanjana was too ashamed to go back to her father. She had already resided with Surya for a long time, and her body temperature was warm. So, she went to the Himalayas to live alone. Still, she was afraid that someone might recognize her there and decided to change her form to that of a mare.

As time went on, Surya's anger dissipated, and he became calm. Thoughts of Sanjana flooded his mind. 'I think there was a genuine reason for the cloning—my heat is unbearable. I maintain my intensity all day. Perhaps I should have had a conversation with Sanjana instead of just expecting her to adjust to me. Maybe I can still change—I can be gentle in the mornings, attain my maximum temperature gradually by noon and reduce it towards the evening, finally retiring for the night. Surely Sanjana can live with me comfortably then.'

Convinced that this was the right move, Surya went in search of her. He could not find her anywhere, but since he was the sun god, he could see everything in the world. Eventually, he learnt that she had transformed into a mare that lived in the Himalayas. Off he went to locate her, disguised as a horse.

When Sanjana laid eyes on him, she saw through the disguise and knew that it was her husband. They spoke openly, and Surya shared his thoughts. They finally came to an understanding and decided to live in the Himalayas for some time.

Soon, Sanjana had twin horses called the Ashwini Kumars (from the term *ashwa*, meaning 'horse' in Sanskrit) and the couple returned to their home. These twins grew up to become physicians in the heavens and were the main controllers of the horses yoked to Surya's golden chariot.

The Ashwini Kumars arrive in the morning as rays and go to work. It is believed that they are the early sun rays that are helpful in curing skin diseases.

The Seven Fierce Mothers

If you visit the temples in the south that were built by the Chola dynasty, you will come across similar-sized statues of seven women, all in a sitting position known as the Lalita Asana, along with different weapons near the sanctum. These statues are known as Saptamatrikas—the seven mothers—who represent divine Shakti, or energy. Their names are: Brahmi, Vaishnavi, Kaatyayini, Indrani, Kaumari, Varahi and Chamunda. If there is an eighth statue, it depicts Yogishwari or Saraswati.

Brahmi is the counterpart of Brahma, and she is often portrayed as having four faces, sitting on a lotus. She is usually dressed in yellow and holds a kamandalu in one hand and a japamala in the other.

Vaishnavi, or Lakshmi, holds a conch and a discus in her hands, just like her male counterpart, Vishnu.

Kaatyayini, or Rudrani, the female form of Shiva, holds a trident in her hand.

Indrani, Indra's counterpart, carries the thunderbolt weapon known as the Vajrayudha.

The six-faced and pale-complexioned Kaumari boasts a peacock as her vehicle and carries the arms of the god of war, Karthikeyan.

Varahi's body is dark, and she has the face of a boar, just like Varaha. She carries a sword and is usually found under a Kalpaka tree.

Chamunda is the popular Chamundeshwari, a goddess in a red sari, wearing a garland of monster faces, carrying a skull and a trident in her hands with a demon depicted at her feet.

The story of the Saptamatrikas arises from different puranas. It is said that the seven mothers were created with the help of Shiva during his battle with Andhakasura. Whenever Shiva inflicted wounds upon Andhaka, his duplicate sprang up with each drop of his spilled blood that touched the ground. This led to the creation of thousands of Andhakas, leaving Shiva to battle with more and more of the same asura. To stop the flow of blood, Shiva created the goddess Yogishwari from the flames coming out of his mouth. The gods, who were watching, decided to assist Shiva, and so, they created their goddess counterparts who could carry and fight with their weapons. Thus, a brigade of seven mothers, headed by Yogishwari, was formed. Together, they stopped Andhaka's blood from falling on the earth by drinking it instead. Shortly thereafter, Shiva defeated the demon.

These goddesses are worshipped all over India, especially in Odisha and West Bengal, where their painted representations are found, as opposed to the sculptures that are often found in the southern parts of the country.

The Weight of a Leaf

The Parijata tree was one of the gifts received during the churning of the ocean. Eventually, it was planted in Indra's royal garden. It boasted unusual white flowers with red stalks that bloomed early in the morning, much before the first rays of the sun. Once the sun's light hit the flowers on the tree, the flowers fell to the ground.

One day, Krishna and his wife Satyabhama went to visit Indra, who was very happy to see them. The king of the gods treated them as his special guests. Indra's wife, Shachi, showed Satyabhama the garden and pointed out the Parijata flowers. Instantly, Satyabhama was smitten by their beauty and fragrance.

When she got a chance, Satyabhama said to Krishna, 'Let's take a branch from this tree to our home. What do you think, dear husband?'

'Let us not ask too much of our host,' he responded, and with that, he ended the conversation.

When they came back home, Satyabhama found herself constantly thinking about the wonderful flowers.

A few days later, Indra sent a few Parijata flowers as a gift to Krishna, who received them in his other wife Rukmini's chambers. He gave the flowers to her.

The wandering and nosy sage Narada observed this and quietly made his way to Satyabhama's chambers. 'Tell me,' he asked Satyabhama, 'do you think Krishna loves all his eight wives equally?'

Satyabhama was aware of Narada's reputation for causing misunderstandings, so she said proudly, 'No, he does not. He loves me the most.'

Narada grinned. 'If that is so, innocent one, then how is it that I saw Krishna give Parijata flowers to Rukmini? The flowers have just come from Indra's abode.'

Satyabhama became furious and deeply upset. 'Krishna knows how I love those flowers! But he's given them to Rukmini! How can he love her more than me?' she thought. Bidding farewell to Narada, she went to a special room built for the queens to express their anger. There, they usually removed their jewellery, left their hair open and slept on the bare ground. Kaikeyi had done so in the Ramayana, and Satyabhama followed suit.

Krishna, who knew what had occurred, pretended to be ignorant. He knocked on the door of the special room. When she didn't respond, he said, 'Bhama, please open the door.'

Satyabhama was still angry and decided to annoy her husband. 'Who is it?' she asked. 'It is the middle of the night, and I don't open the door for strangers.'

'I am that great fish that saved the world and the great Vedas,' he replied. Krishna was referring to himself as Vishnu in his first avatar—the fish Matsya.

'Well, you have lived in the water for ages, so you must stink of the sea. I cannot open the door for you.'

Krishna continued, 'I am also the one who took the burden of the weight of the universe during the churning of the ocean. Now, open the door.' He was speaking of the turtle Kurma, the second avatar of Vishnu.

'We don't have any weight-bearing work in the palace. Go back to where you came from,' came the feisty response.

'I am the wild boar who killed the mighty Hiranyaksha and saved the world. Open, Bhama.'

Satyabhama was equally adamant. She said, 'Wild boars are very dangerous. How do you expect me to open the door for you? After all, I am a delicate woman.'

'I understood the plight of Prahlada and came for him as the mighty lion-faced man. Open the door.'

'I am not scared of the lion or its ferociousness, and yet, I will not let you in,' said Satyabhama.

Krishna smiled, enjoying the conversation. 'I am the one who came in the form of a small, young and intelligent boy to conquer Bali. Come now, don't be stubborn.'

'The truth is that you cheated the great emperor Bali with your intelligence, and later, you became his security guard. You can't be trusted! I am not going to open the door for such a being.'

Finally, he said, 'O Bhama, I am your loving husband, Krishna. Will you open the door for me now?'

Bhama opened the door. She wasn't angry any more but still jealous that she had not been given the Parijata flowers. 'If you truly love me, then make sure that you plant the Parijata tree in my garden. I don't care what you need to do.

Until I see the tree here, I will not eat or drink,' she said to her husband.

Meanwhile, Narada was up to no good. He went to Indra and said, 'Krishna is going to request you for the Parijata tree. His wife Satyabhama is hell-bent on possessing it.'

Indra became upset. 'How can Satyabhama ask for a heavenly tree to be sent to earth? If Krishna asks for it, I will give it to him, but on the condition that the branch I give will not yield any fruit when planted on earth.'

As expected, Krishna came to visit Indra. He said to his friend, 'Bhama wants this heavenly tree. I know that this is an improper request, but perhaps you can spare one for her?'

Indra warned him, 'I will give you a branch that will grow into a tree. However, the tree will never bear any fruit.'

Krishna accepted the condition and brought the branch back to Satyabhama. She was extremely happy and planted it in the corner of her garden that shared a wall with Rukmini's lawn. She thought, 'Rukmini had those flowers only for a day, but soon, I will have them every day. Krishna does love me more!'

The tree grew, and Satyabhama looked after it very well. But with the passing of time, she noticed that not a single flower bloomed or fell in her side of the garden. The tree was bent towards Rukmini's side of the wall, with flowering branches coming down her side. Every day, Satyabhama watered the tree, but Rukmini was the one who got the flowers. It made Satyabhama furious.

The next time Narada visited, she asked him, 'O sage, I love Krishna more than anyone else. He got me the tree

that I wanted, but only Rukmini is benefitting from it. What is the meaning of this?'

The sage smiled. 'It is true that you love Krishna, but Rukmini worships him. Her love is pure and without expectation, and that virtue attracts Krishna more. That is why Krishna is also known as Rukmini Vallabha—the husband of Rukmini.'

Satyabhama finally realized her folly.

Months passed, and Narada again visited Satyabhama one day. He looked tired.

Satyabhama asked him, 'What is the matter? Why are you so weary today?'

'O Satyabhama, I am just coming from Rukmini's home. She is the chief queen and a princess. Her heart is large, indeed. She gave me some charity for the welfare of her husband, and the bag was quite heavy. That is the cause of my weariness,' responded Narada, knowing it would provoke Satyabhama.

Instantly, Satyabhama became jealous and angry. 'Dear sage, I may not be a princess, but my father is a rich man too. I can also give charity for the sake of my husband.'

'Yes, your father owned Shamantakamani, and you are no less than a princess,' said Narada.

'Money is not the problem, Satyabhama. Will you give me whatever I want? Perhaps it will make you better than Rukmini and bring you more fame.'

'Ask me for anything, dear sage. I will give it to you. I promise,' insisted Satyabhama. 'Come on, ask away,' she added impatiently.

'Well, then give me your husband as charity. Rukmini will never do so,' said Narada.

'Of course! A promise is a promise,' said Satyabhama quickly, without thinking.

Immediately, Narada called Krishna and informed him about the charity.

Krishna smiled and said, 'I do not exist in my own right. Whatever my wife says, I will agree to.'

Narada asked for water, and without a second thought, Satyabhama completed the custom with water and tulsi and gave away Krishna as *dana*, or charity.

Narada turned to Krishna and said, 'Now remove your jewels and expensive robes and change into ordinary ones. Here, carry my bag and follow me wherever I go.'

Satyabhama was alarmed. 'Don't speak to my husband like this! He is not your slave. Why will he follow you around? You don't even own a place for him to stay. Then who will take care of him?'

'You have no right to ask me such questions,' said Narada firmly. 'You have given Krishna to me in charity—he belongs to me now. I am his master. It is my wish to take him wherever I please. I may or may not send him back, depending on my desire and the work to be done.'

That was the moment Satyabhama realized her mistake. In a fit of jealousy and anger, she had given her husband to a sage to please her ego.

The news quickly reached Krishna's other wives, and they came looking for Satyabhama. Some were filled with panic, some were crying and some were livid. All of them scolded her, 'How dare you give our husband away?

He is a living person and not an object. Moreover, he doesn't belong to you alone—he also belongs to his parents, his other wives and his devotees. Krishna belongs to everyone. What have you done?'

Satyabhama became afraid and begged Narada, 'O sage, please forgive me. I have made a terrible mistake. I alone do not own Krishna. Please give him back to us.'

'I understand the plight of the other wives,' began Narada. 'I will consider their pain and return Krishna. However, once dana is given, it cannot be taken back. So, I must receive something else. Satyabhama, perhaps you can give me gold worth Krishna's weight, and I will let him go.' He looked at Krishna.

Krishna gave a mysterious smile. Relieved, Satyabhama was confident in her reply. 'Of course! I am the daughter of Satrajitha, so giving you gold is not a problem for me at all.'

Satyabhama called out for the largest weighing scale and made Krishna sit on one of the pans. Then she began adding gold on the other pan. But Krishna's scale still touched the ground. After she had finished placing all the gold she had, she started placing numerous heavy gold vessels she had received from her father. Still, she couldn't match Krishna's weight. Then she removed all the jewellery from her body and placed it, but the scale showed no sign of balancing the two pans. At the end, Satyabhama was left with nothing.

Everyone was astonished at this turn of events.

Narada remarked, 'You have not fulfilled my condition, Satyabhama. I have to keep Krishna with me. O Gopala, get up and follow me.'

Satyabhama looked at Krishna helplessly.

Krishna smiled at Narada, who then turned to Satyabhama and said, 'I will give you one more chance. You may call Rukmini and seek her assistance.'

At first, Satyabhama resisted. 'How can Rukmini bail me out of this situation?' she thought. 'She has no wealth at all! How can she help me with extra gold? But I have no other option, and I really want Krishna back.' So, she turned to Rukmini and asked, 'Sister, will you come and help me?'

Rukmini went to the garden nearby and came back with one tulsi leaf. She said, 'If my devotion for Krishna is true, then the weighing scale will mark the pans as equal now.'

Rukmini carefully placed the leaf on the pan carrying the gold, and to everyone's pleasant surprise, the pan lifted to the exact height of Krishna's pan—the scales were finally balanced.

'You may come down now, Krishna,' said Narada. Then he said to Satyabhama, 'Devotion is more important than possession. Rukmini loves Krishna unconditionally, and that is why the pans became equal in weight.'

Satyabhama bent her head in shame, vowing never to forget this valuable lesson.

The Temple without a Deity

There once lived a tribal chief named Viswavasu, who worshipped the statue of the powerful wish-fulfilling god Nila Madhava. Viswavasu's tribe was located near the bluish grey stone range of mountains named Niladri, or Nilachala, in today's state of Odisha.

In those days, Odisha was known as Kalinga, and the vast empire was ruled by a king named Indradyumna. When the king heard of the powerful presence of the god in the statue, he wanted to install the deity in his kingdom. And so, he sent word to Viswavasu.

The tribal chief, however, flatly refused. 'This is our god, and we cannot send him away,' he said.

Indradyumna was desperate to obtain the deity and assigned the task to his smart younger brother, Vidyapati.

Disguised as a priest, Vidyapati made his way to the tribe and learnt that the statue was securely kept in a cave in the deepest part of the forest. Viswavasu was aware of the king's yearning for the deity and visited the god with utmost secrecy. Vidyapati tried his best to find the location of the statue but to no avail. The tribal chief was too smart, and the details of the deity's exact location had been told only to a few trusted men.

Vidyapati thought, 'I must find a way to get into the inner circle of the chief's men.' He began devising a plan.

Viswavasu had a beautiful daughter named Lalita, and the king's brother knew that this could be a way to get to the sculpture of Nila Madhava. So, Vidyapati charmed Lalita so much that she fell in love with him and insisted on marrying him. Viswavasu was a loving father and gave in to his daughter's request. Soon, the two were married.

Still, Vidyapati didn't get an opportunity to see the deity. Time passed, and in his new setting, Vidyapati noticed that his father-in-law disappeared every fortnight and came back the next morning. Sensing an opportunity, Vidyapati said to his wife, 'Lalita, I am your husband, so I would like to worship the family god. Will you take me to the holy Nila Madhava?'

Innocent Lalita believed her husband and approached her father. At first, he refused her request. But Lalita persisted until he finally said, 'I will blindfold your husband and take him to the deity. Then I will remove the blindfold and he can worship the lord. After that, I will blindfold him again and bring him back here.'

Vidyapati was ecstatic at the news. This was his chance. The next fortnight, when Viswavasu took him to the cave blindfolded, Vidyapati carried a bag of mustard seeds with a hole in the bottom. The seeds dropped slowly to the ground, all the way to the cave. There, Vidyapati worshipped the deity and came back as planned. Then, he waited for the season of rain that was about to come.

Soon, with the heavy rainfall, the mustard seeds began to germinate, and yellow flowers danced in the air. When the time was right, Vidyapati followed the mustard plants, reached the cave, stole Nila Madhava and hurriedly went back to the city of Puri.

As soon as King Indradyumna heard the news of his brother's arrival, he went to him, hoping to see the lord. But alas! The statue was nowhere to be found! It seemed to have disappeared.

The king was utterly disappointed. 'I will not stop until I see the deity,' he cried out. 'I will fast until death.'

Suddenly, a celestial voice boomed, 'The statue is hidden in the sand. You may view it tomorrow.'

The following day, at the break of dawn, the king ran to the beach. However, he saw only a log of wood. The celestial voice again instructed the king, 'Pray to Vishwakarma, the architect of the heavens. He will help you.'

And so, Indradyumna began his prayers in earnest. While he was praying, a mysterious old man arrived. He had an ethereal presence and a calm demeanour. The man told Indradyumna that he would convert the divine log of wood into three statues of Jagannath (a form of Vishnu), Balabhadra (Krishna's brother, Balarama) and Subhadra (Krishna's sister).

However, the old man set a condition. 'I will help you, dear king, but I must do my work with the door closed. Nobody must disturb me until I am done. I shall open the door myself once the task is complete.'

King Indradyumna was ecstatic and agreed to the condition.

The work began, and a few months passed. Neither did the door open even once nor was there a request for food. What's more—there was no sound from the inside! Indradyumna and his wife, the queen, became anxious. 'What if the old man has died?' the queen wondered.

'Let's open the door,' she said to the king.

At first, the king resisted, but after much coaxing, he gave in. The soldiers forced their way inside the room and found that the statues were not yet complete. The king, who had accompanied his men, saw that the old man was no longer there, but instead, saw Vishwakarma. He instantly realized that it was the architect of the heavens who had been the one working on the statues.

'Your foolishness has forced me to leave the work half-done. The statues will now remain like this with no hands,' thundered Vishwakarma. 'However, Lord Jagannath, being as compassionate as he is, will still bless the kingdom.'

Vishwakarma disappeared and the half-made wooden statues remained in the inner sanctum of the room.

Today, if you visit the Jagannath Temple in Odisha, you will see the three deities without their hands.

Though the statues were incomplete, Indradyumna was still very grateful that the lord was ensuring the protection of everybody in his kingdom. He declared, 'Whoever rules the kingdom of Kalinga must remember that he is not the owner of the empire. The owner is Lord Jagannath, and we are his servants. To showcase his genuine sentiment, each king must clean the chariot himself before the annual chariot festival, which we shall call the Rath Yatra.'

The generations that came after Indradyumna followed his instructions. Among these rulers was a brave prince, Purushottama Deva, who was a powerful and just leader of the empire. The prince's royal family considered Jagannath to be their master. In order to show his humility and obedience, the prince would sweep the chariot with a golden broom every year, indicating to the world and his subjects that he was a mere servant of the lord.

In time, he heard of the beautiful Padmavati, the princess of Kanchipuram, and through his officials sent word of a marriage proposal to her. The princess, however, became enraged and declared in open court, 'How can I marry a royal scavenger who sweeps the ground with a golden broom?'

The news reached the prince instantly, and he decided to teach the princess a lesson. He invaded Kanchipuram, defeated the king, imprisoned Padmavati and brought her back to Puri. He took nothing else from the kingdom.

Back in the capital, and without even seeing the princess, the prince instructed his chief minister, 'Please ensure that this arrogant princess is married to a scavenger as soon as possible.'

Luckily for him, the chief minister of Kalinga was a wise old man. He knew that sometimes people spoke and acted in anger without understanding the consequences. Padmavati had surely made an error by looking down upon the prince in public, but she also did not deserve such a dire punishment. So, the chief minister hid her from the prince and kept her safely. He taught her how to be modest and merciful to others. Over time, Padmavati learnt much from the wise man and regretted her vain behaviour.

The next year at the chariot festival, the prince arrived in a spotless white outfit, armed with a golden broom. As always, he began cleaning the chariot speedily. Suddenly, a beautiful maiden approached him, and before he could gather his thoughts, she garlanded him.

The prince stopped in his tracks. He asked her, 'Who are you, young maiden? How dare you garland me?'

The princess said in a shy and quiet voice, 'I am your wife now since I have completed one of the ceremonies necessary for a marriage.'

The prince was furious.

Just then, the chief minister intervened, 'Sire, this is Padmavati, the princess of Kanchipuram.'

The king had almost forgotten about her. 'I told you to marry her off to a scavenger,' he yelled at the minister. 'Why isn't she married yet?'

The chief minister was calm. 'But, sire, I have fulfilled your instructions. You are carrying a golden broom, and you have just swept the chariot. You are, indeed, a scavenger to God, and now she is married to you.'

The prince was surprised by this turn of events. He realized that the chief minister had made the right decision, and he pardoned Padmavati.

The minister added, 'O dear prince! You must never do anything in anger or in a hurry. Important decisions that affect people's lives must be deliberated over with care and concern. May Lord Jagannath protect both of you and may you live happily ever after.'

Even today, the head of the royal family in Puri cleans the chariot every year with a golden broom at the beginning of the Rath Yatra. There are three chariots in the yatra: one for Krishna, one for Balabhadra and one for Subhadra. The wooden deities are placed on the chariots and taken to the end of the road to their aunt's house—Gundecha Temple—where the statues are installed for a week before being returned to their original home. This is the only temple in India that doesn't have its deities for an entire week!

Soldiers in the Elephant's Stomach

This tale is from *Swapna Vasavadatta*, or Vasavadatta's Dream, a Sanskrit play written by an ancient Indian playwright named Bhasa.

King Udayana of Vatsadesha was young, handsome, compassionate and pious. He was known for his mastery of his veena called Ghoshavati. He was so good at the instrument that when he played in the forest, elephants came to hear the music.

The king had lost his parents and relied on the advice of his extraordinary chief minister, Yaugandharayana. The minister was aware that other kings kept a close eye on the kingdom because of its young and inexperienced ruler, so he would frequently tell Udayana, 'O sire! I appreciate your love for the fine arts, but you are also a king. Please keep your focus only on the welfare of your subjects and maintain diplomatic relations with your neighbouring kingdoms.'

King Udayana, however, wouldn't always listen.

One of the neighbouring kings, Pradyota, the ruler of Avanti, had a beautiful daughter named Vasavadatta.

She excelled at almost everything. Pradyota was in search of a suitable groom for his daughter, but nobody was a match for her skills. People would often comment to the king, 'Only Udayana is a fit husband for her, but he doesn't want to get married. He is happy with his veena and barely has time for anything else.'

After some thought, Pradyota hatched a plan. He called the most skilled carpenters in his kingdom and asked them to make a huge lifelike elephant that was hollow inside. After it was built, Pradyota asked his soldiers to get inside it and placed the elephant in a corner of his kingdom, right next to the border of Udayana's kingdom. At the same time, he spread a rumour in both the kingdoms that a gigantic elephant has entered the forests of Avanti and is causing chaos among the subjects.

Soon, the news reached Udayana who was about to depart to the forest to play the veena. Yaugandharayana stopped him. 'O king! There is something fishy about the news we have received. I haven't heard any of our men confirming the existence of an enormous elephant. Our people haven't reported anything unusual on our side of the kingdom. If the news is true, why isn't there more panic around it, and why hasn't Pradyota done anything about it yet? I fear that there is something else behind this. I will advise you not to go to your usual spot in the forest today. But if you still insist, I will have to ensure that you take a few of our best soldiers with you.'

King Udayana was adamant about going to the forest. Half-heartedly, he agreed to take some soldiers with him on the minister's insistence.

Once he reached the forest, he began playing the veena, Ghoshavati, and many elephants came to listen. Just then, he noticed a big elephant in the distance, moving away from the music. He said to his soldiers, 'Never has an elephant walked away from me. On the contrary, the wildest of elephants come and surrender to the music without harming me. I think that that big elephant is not coming here because of your presence. So go away. This is an order.'

Reluctantly, the soldiers retreated and watched the king from afar. King Udayana took his veena and entered Avanti's side of the forest. He saw the elephant, but it continued moving away from him, despite the music. King Udayana couldn't understand what was wrong. He thought that the elephant's behaviour was an insult to Ghoshavati. So, he followed the elephant farther into the forest. When he was deep inside the kingdom of Avanti, the soldiers emerged from the hollow stomach of the elephant and imprisoned him. With due honour, they presented him to Pradyota.

King Pradyota was charmed by Udayana. He knew that if he requested Udayana to marry his daughter, the king would refuse. So, he decided to trick him and made sure that he didn't treat Udayana like a prisoner. On the contrary, Pradyota treated him like an important guest and said, 'I apologize for bringing you here this way, dear Udayana. I have an ugly and short-tempered daughter who is incapable of learning anything. I will gladly release you if you teach her the veena. You have a great reputation as a wonderful teacher, and the veena listens to you, as do wild animals. I am certain that my daughter will be able to learn something from you too. But remember that there will always be a curtain separating the two of you during the classes, and you must not see her face. Otherwise, her ugliness will cause you to flee from here.'

Later, Pradyota called his daughter, Vasavadatta, to his private chambers and said, 'I have just taken an arrogant king as my prisoner. He knows the veena fairly well, but he is very ugly and short-tempered. I thought that you could take advantage of his presence while he is here and learn the veena, but please don't ever look at him or you will run away at the sight of his grotesque face. Keep your focus on the education he is giving you—respect that and don't worry about the physical form. A guru is, after all, a great man!'

Thus, he lowered their expectations. Vasavadatta and Udayana began their music lessons together in a private room, a curtain separating them.

Udayana soon realized that Vasavadatta was a sharp student. She was learning fast.

One day, she played an obviously wrong note during her lesson. Udayana became upset. 'O princess, you are not only ugly and arrogant but also have not practised properly since our last session. Beauty may be in God's hands, but the least you can do is focus on the pursuit of knowledge.'

Vasavadatta became furious. 'Horrid king, you must learn how to respect a princess. Besides, you are still my father's prisoner. I agree that I made a mistake, but it was because I was in a hurry to come here and did not practise today. A teacher should be compassionate and guide his students well. You don't seem to have that qualification, along with a lack of good looks.'

An exchange of words ensued, and, in anger, they walked up to the curtain and the princess pulled at it. Suddenly, they

found themselves staring at each other. They were both extraordinarily good-looking and fell in love instantly. This had been Pradyota's plan all along.

From that day on, Udayana longed to see Vasavadatta every day. Teaching the veena was forgotten, and instead, they talked, walked in the gardens and spent time together.

Soon, Udayana wanted to marry her and go back to his kingdom, but as the king's prisoner, he felt ashamed to ask Pradyota for his daughter's hand in marriage. He managed to send a secret message to his chief minister, Yaugandharayana, who had been busy holding the fort in the king's absence, conveying his desire to elope with Princess Vasavadatta.

One night, Yaugandharayana sent a female elephant named Bhadra to rescue the king. King Pradyota learnt of the plan but decided to do nothing until the next morning. Princess Vasavadatta and King Udayana ran away from the palace and Bhadra brought them back to Vatsadesha.

The next day, Pradyota pretended to be tremendously upset about his daughter's elopement with the royal prisoner and sent a few soldiers to track them down, knowing that by the time the men did so, the couple would be in Kausambi, the capital of Vatsa, which is called Allahabad today. As predicted, the soldiers came back empty-handed.

King Udayana in a quick but grand ceremony married Vasavadatta. The couple led a blissful life together. King Udayana was still the same, for he hardly went to the court, but now, he spent most of his time with Vasavadatta. Their love and devotion were mutual. Many times, Vasavadatta herself said to her husband that he should spend more time on his royal duties, but Udayana did not change his ways.

Time passed and Yaugandharayana grew extremely worried about the future of the kingdom. One day, when Udayana was away from the palace, the minister visited the queen in her chambers and explained the political situation to her. 'Queen Vasavadatta, I request you to please understand my dilemma. We are a small kingdom, and our neighbours are mighty and powerful. If the circumstances were different, the king would have been advised to marry princesses from our bigger neighbouring states for diplomatic reasons, and not for love.

'One of our neighbours, the kingdom of Magadha, is ready to invade us. If that happens, we will all perish. The princess of Magadha is Padmavati, and I recommend that our king marry her to keep the peace. Even if we approach the king of Magadha for his daughter's hand for a second marriage, he may be hesitant because your love for Udayana and his affection for you are so well-known. Any king would think deeply before such a marriage for his daughter. I urge you only to think about what I have said today.'

Vasavadatta became concerned after Yaugandharayana's departure. She was a princess herself and knew that royal marriages were often arranged for the benefit of kingdoms. The unusual challenge she saw ahead was convincing her husband to get married again. It is very hard for a woman to tell her husband to marry another, even though the times were such that it was considered a king's privilege and right to do so.

Soon, Vasavadatta made up her mind and spoke openly to the king, along with Yaugandharayana, who supported her and insisted on the importance of such a political marriage for the welfare of the subjects.

Udayana flatly refused. 'As long as you are with me, Vasavadatta, I cannot have any other woman as my wife.'

The next day, Yaugandharayana came up with another plan and shared it with Vasavadatta. 'Queen, I have thought of a different approach to solve our problem. The king says that he will not get married again, presumably, for as long as you are alive. So, let's pretend for some time that you are dead. Once the king gets married to Padmavati, you can return safely. Udayana's love for you is eternal, and no one feels it more than the two of you. What do you think? Will you help me with this plan?'

At first, Vasavadatta was taken aback. But the more she thought about it, the more she realized that Yaugandharayana's plan was the only option to protect the kingdom and the people. As a queen, it was her duty to do so. It was hard for her to leave Udayana, but she knew that it had to be done for the greater good.

Within a week, the plan was to reach its culmination. Queen Vasavadatta, along with Yaugandharayana, made a plan to visit Lavanika for a festival. King Udayana also wanted to accompany them, but the queen did not allow him to do so. Sometime later, news reached Udayana that there had been a terrible fire at the festivities and that his queen, Vasavadatta, had died in it.

Udayana could not contain his grief. He chastised himself. 'Why didn't I accompany Vasavadatta? At least we could have died together. It would have been much better than suffering through a life like this.'

He cursed his minister Yaugandharayana. 'Why didn't he protect my queen?' But it was too late. The king knew that nothing could be done.

Stealthily, Yaugandharayana took Vasavadatta to his home, and she lived there, hidden from everyone.

After several months, Yaugandharayana conveniently brought the proposal of Padmavati to the king once again. Reluctantly, Udayana agreed for political reasons, and since he no longer had Queen Vasavadatta by his side.

Soon, the wedding preparations began, and the bride's party arrived. In the minister's house, Queen Vasavadatta became restless and couldn't stay away any longer. She felt an impulsive desire to see her husband once before he got married again.

One afternoon, Udayana was asleep in the chambers adjacent to the wedding hall.

Vasavadatta disguised herself in an ordinary sari and covered her head and face. Silently, she approached his room.

As she entered, she found Udayana muttering in his sleep, 'O Vasavadatta, if only you would not have died in Lavanika, we would have been so happy. My life is incomplete without you . . .'

Vasavadatta could not control her tears. She went up to him and whispered, 'I am always with you.' She took a last look at the king and quickly walked away from his chambers.

The king woke with a start. He called Yaugandharayana and said, 'Vasavadatta is not dead. She is alive. I saw her in my dream! I feel it in my bones that she lives. She visited me in my chambers and spoke to me while dressed in an ordinary sari. Why don't you stop the impending wedding and search for her instead?'

Yaugandharayana smiled. 'Sire, Queen Vasavadatta is not alive. You dreamt of her because of your intense love for her. This is just a dream—swapna Vasavadatta.'

Meanwhile, Vasavadatta decided to see the bride from a distance. Everybody was busy getting her ready.

A lady-in-waiting saw Vasavadatta and mistook her for a flower woman. 'Make two garlands for the wedding,' they instructed her and ordered her to sit down to complete the task as soon as possible. Vasavadatta began making two garlands for her husband's wedding using her unusual technique of making garlands called *koutukamala*. Her sadness grew deeper with the completion of each garland, and she couldn't hold back her tears by the time she was done.

During the wedding ceremony, the garlands were exchanged, and the couple was officially married.

Vasavadatta stood behind a curtain, her eyes brimming with tears.

Udayana traced his fingers along the garland around his neck. He realized something and said aloud, 'This garland surely has Vasavadatta's touch. No one else can do this because I was the one to teach her koutukamala. She is alive, I am sure, and now, I want to see her desperately.'

Yaugandharayana came forward and said, 'Sire, it was all my doing. Please pardon me. The queen is indeed alive and well and agreed to do what she did to save the kingdom from invasion. Please forgive both of us.'

As the minister finished, Vasavadatta emerged from behind the curtain. When the king saw her, his happiness knew no bounds, and he pardoned his well-meaning minister.

The new bride, Padmavati, approached Vasavadatta and bowed to her, accepting her as a sister.

With renewed understanding and wisdom, Udayana lived with the two queens happily ever after.

This well-known drama in Sanskrit literature is considered to be a gem of the language. The pure affection between Vasavadatta and Udayana was used as an inspiration for future literature in Sanskrit.

The Forgotten Wife

Vachaspati Mishra, a man of outstanding academic calibre, was born in the Mithila region of Magadha (today's Bihar) sometime between 900 and 980 CE. His single mother, Vatsala, faced a lot of hardship while raising him.

When Vachaspati became a young man, she thought about getting him married. Soon, she found a young bride for him from the neighbouring village and spoke to her son about her.

'My sole purpose is to write a bhashya, a commentary, on Vedanta Sutras or Brahma Sutras. The scriptures are very important and dear to me, and the commentary will be my service to the country,' Vachaspati said to his mother. 'Once I start writing a bhashya, I will be immersed in it and won't be able to perform the duties of a husband or a father. You know that, Mother. Please convey this to the bride's side. But tell me, Amma, after hearing all this, do you still want me to get married?'

Vatsala was surprised by her son's decision. She felt that it was futile for him to get married and ruin a girl's life. Hesitantly, she shared her son's opinion with the bride's father. Everyone was shocked. The girl's father appreciated Vachaspati's frankness, humility and honesty, and he asked his daughter for her opinion. The young girl said, 'I will marry him and abide by his condition.'

Vachaspati was glad. He realized that the girl must be special because she had chosen him despite knowing what difficulties lay ahead of her.

The couple was wed on the auspicious day of Vyasa Purnima. It was also the most wonderful time for him to start writing a bhashya. The moment he reached home after the wedding, he sat in the veranda and began writing. Days turned into nights. His mother, Vatsala, brought him whatever he wanted, while his wife observed.

Months, seasons and years passed, and Vachaspati remained focused on his work. After a few years, his mother died. Now, his wife took over the care for her husband, who had very few physical needs—a bath, food and a few hours of sleep.

For years, she served him without any expectation while staying out of his sight. The palm leaves he wrote on were always at hand, the lamp was well oiled for the night, his clothes were washed, fresh food was always served on time and he was never disturbed while he worked. Vachaspati never thought about how well looked after he was.

One night, he finally completed his commentary. Vachaspati put his pen down and stood up. He was in ecstasy! At last, his life's work was done.

In the dim light, he saw an old woman sleeping in the corner of the room.

At the slight noise, she stirred from her sleep.

Vachaspati asked her, 'Old lady, who are you? What are you doing in my room at this time?'

'I am your wife. You married me decades ago. All this time, you have been so busy writing that I never disturbed you.'

Vachaspati was stunned. He vaguely remembered his beautiful young bride, who was now apparently this old woman. Had so much time truly passed? Then he saw his reflection in an oil pot and almost didn't recognize himself—it was the face of an elderly man.

Vachaspati went to his wife and saw her hands. He recalled that they were the same ones that would come near him to serve his food and fill the oil in his lamp. He was familiar with the hands, but not her face. Tears began flowing down his cheeks. 'I have been unfair to you. I have not fulfilled any of my duties towards you, but you have. I am fortunate to have a woman like you who has given me so much unconditional love, been patient with me and treated me with a large heart. You are truly exceptional. May I know your name?'

The old woman smiled. She said, 'I accepted your condition and got married to you, dear husband. I know that when you have achieved such great heights in philosophy, you will need someone to look after you with kindness and affection, and I have done all that I could. My name is Bhamati.'

Vachaspati nodded at her and went back to his desk.

He took the quill and opened to the first page of his finished bhashya. It had been kept vacant for a suitable title. He wrote with his trembling hand—Bhamati.

Vachaspati turned to his wife and said, 'I have named this work after you. Whoever reads this may or may not remember me, but they will definitely remember you. Behind every great work of a man, there always exists the unconditional love from a woman who deserves more recognition than the man himself. You will be the best example in history to convey to the world that women are much greater than these works.'

In the present times, we don't know much about Vachaspati Mishra, but everybody knows about the Bhamati school of Advaita Vedanta. Today, Bhamati's name remains synonymous with great patience and unconditional love.